"You don't think she was still alive when he . . . did that? Took her heart?"

"Hmm?" Slick mumbled, opening the massive wound even more to give clear access to the entire chest cavity.

Jenna realized it was her cue. She reached inside the girl's chest to begin removing the organs as the M.E. started to make his cuts.

"Why would he take her heart out?" she asked, more to herself than to the doctors.

"A souvenir?" Slick suggested. "There are many stories, most apocryphal but some true, about serial killers keeping trophies from their victims."

"You mean he *kept* it?" she asked, holding the girl's lungs in her hands. "Her heart?"

"It wasn't found at the crime scene," Dyson told her.

Jenna suddenly felt very cold inside. She went over to the scale to weigh the girl's lungs, but her mind had already left the room. As she looked down at the glazed eyes of the dead girl on that cold steel table, she was filled, suddenly, with the certainty that it wasn't over.

Someone who could do something like this wasn't going to stop after one.

christopher golden

THIEF of HEARTS

A *Body of Evidence*
thriller starring Jenna Blake

AN ARCHWAY PAPERBACK
Published by POCKET BOOKS
New York London Toronto Sydney Tokyo Singapore

This book is a work of fiction. Names, characters, places and incidents are products of the author's imagination or are used fictitiously. Any resemblance to actual events or locales or persons, living or dead, is entirely coincidental.

AN ARCHWAY PAPERBACK *Original*

An Archway Paperback published by
POCKET BOOKS, a division of Simon & Schuster Inc.
1230 Avenue of the Americas, New York, NY 10020

Copyright © 1999 by Christopher Golden

ISBN: 0-671-03493-6

First Archway Paperback printing August 1999

10 9 8 7 6 5 4 3 2 1

AN ARCHWAY PAPERBACK and colophon are registered trademarks of Simon & Schuster Inc.

Front cover illustration by Kamil Vojnar

Printed in the U.S.A.

for Lisa Scarlett and Pam Wetzel

acknowledgments

Thanks, as always, to Connie and the boys, to my agent, Lori Perkins, my friend and editor, Lisa Clancy, and her heroic assistant, Liz Shiflett. Very special thanks to Captain Thomas M. Meaney, USMC, Special Agent Jeff Thurman, FBI, and Dr. Cheryl Hanau.

Working on this series, I find names and faces popping into my head all the time. What better place, then, to thank them, just for making my time in college such a pleasure? I'm sure I'll forget all kinds of people I should thank, but maybe next time. So thanks and fond thoughts to: Jose Nieto, Lisa DeLissio, Jen Keates, Lisa Scarlett, Pam Wetzel, Steve Eliopoulos, Jean-marc Joseph, Kiera O'Neil, Gerilyn Alfe, Dave Neal, Emmanuel Gardner, Nancy Sali, Margaret Pearce (have I got a story for you, Mags—maybe I'll share it with you one day), Robin Gonci, Helen Nadel, Lisa Boggs, Carol Campagna, Kim Ryan, Jackie Brandolini, Lesley Egler, Amy Zarin, Elaine Casey, Wendy Harrington, Valerie Bolling, Roseanne Brusco, Melissa Bogursky, Paula Odonne, Meta Tjan, Sarah Cion, and Barbra Isenberg.

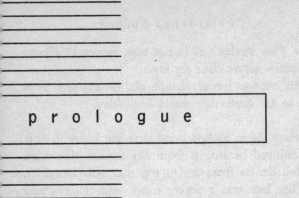

prologue

Murder itself held no pleasure for him. It was what came after—that was what he lived for.

It was just after eight on a Wednesday night. The sky was clear, and the early October breeze blew cold across Harvard Square in Cambridge. The place, he knew, was a mecca for students from Harvard, M.I.T., Somerset, and other area colleges. Even midweek, what surrounded him now was a sea of students, wave after wave of them with their dyed hair, piercings, and torn and droopy clothes. There were plenty of others, as well, kids who were less conspicuous, more conservative. In fact, they were the majority.

But all he saw in the vast sea of flesh were the loud ones, the colorful ones, the ones the others gravitated toward. He was excited by them and thrilled that he had found one with charisma, inner strength, and confi-

1

dence. They wouldn't all be that way. He wasn't allowed to choose—nature chose for him.

This one was special, though, and he was eager to be close to her. Soon, they would be together.

Kelsey Zarin looked good, and she knew it. Still, she enjoyed hearing it from her friends. She wore beaded denim flairs and a top that was too tight, and her hair was a severe mess, with a screaming red strand hanging down in front of her face.

"Hey!"

Kelsey turned at the shout and saw Caitie Abrams, along with a bunch of other people, coming up the stairs from the T station. With a smile and a flap of her arms, Kelsey started toward her friend.

"Dude!" she said, rolling her eyes. "You are *so* late. I told those guys to go on, that we'd find them."

Caitie looked panicked a moment. "You have my ticket, though, right?"

For half a second Kelsey thought about pretending not to have it, but Caitie seemed so totally wigged that Kelsey just nodded and grabbed her by the arm. Greek Tragedy was playing at Delgado's, and they were lucky to have tickets. Even though she wasn't totally into the band, no way was she going to miss a night partying with her friends—not even for Caitie. In fact, if Caitie hadn't shown up in another two minutes, Kelsey would have just bagged on her and given the ticket to some poor lost soul.

Or sold it for fun and profit.

They walked out of the center of the Square and down toward the Charles River. Kelsey was kind of bummed that she hadn't been around before the Square got so commercial. People talked all the time about what it was like before there was a Gap on, like, every corner. Still, it was cool. There were plenty of non-chain businesses and they were fun. There were about a million specialty and used-book shops in Harvard Square, not to mention the best ice cream on God's green earth and some really spicy restaurants.

College was all right, as far as Kelsey was concerned, but without Harvard Square, it would be too boring for words. She was brilliant. She had known that before M.I.T. offered her a free ride for all four years. But she just didn't like to study. Being able to hang in the Square and party with her friends—that was a decent trade-off for studying for a future in physics at NASA, or wherever.

They passed The Garage, and the travel agent where they had that sign that said "Please Go Away," which she'd always liked, and then they were crossing Mt. Auburn Street.

"I'm so psyched for this show," Caitie shouted. "I can't believe I missed that BNL concert last week, but this'll make up for it."

Kelsey raised her eyebrows. She didn't say anything, but she thought, *Just keep telling yourself that. As if.*

Then they were at Delgado's, where there wasn't a line. Anyone with tickets was already inside, and anyone else was just screwed. Back in the eighteen hundreds, Delgado's had been a huge tavern in Harvard Square. Then, in the sixties and seventies, it had become an eccentric little marketplace for weird jewelry and clothes. Sometime in the nineteen eighties it became Delgado's.

And managed to remain cool ever since. If a band was cutting edge, but not popular enough to fill the Orpheum, they played Delgado's. The music was always good, but Greek Tragedy was definitely on the way up, so tonight should be something special.

After they passed their tickets to the bouncer at the door, Kelsey put a hand on Caitie's arm.

"What's up?" Caitie asked and stopped just inside the door, where a dull roar of conversation was building in anticipation of the band.

"You and me," Kelsey said. "We're cool about Ryan, right? I mean, you don't mind if I . . ."

Caitie smiled bitterly and then shrugged. "He didn't want me, Kels. Maybe you'll have more luck."

Kelsey rolled her eyes. "You make it sound so cheap and tawdry."

"There's a reason for that," Catie said, her smile making it clear she wasn't joking.

Kelsey didn't care.

She thought she and Ryan would be good together, and it was obvious he liked her. As long as she had covered her ass with Caitie, she figured it was worth a shot. He was a good guy, and she wanted to spend more time with him.

They shoved their way through the crowd at the bar and into a more open space where there were a bunch of tables and chairs set up. Beyond that were the stage and a small dance floor for people who couldn't sit still. Across the stage was a heavy, old-fashioned velvet curtain, and Kelsey could hear the distant clash of a cymbal and the rumbling thunder of someone testing the drum setup.

She hadn't been all that psyched about seeing Greek Tragedy. They were good, but not as good as her friends thought. But now she was getting psyched—Delgado's was a cool place to be—and she'd be with Ryan.

"There they are," Caitie said and tugged on Kelsey's hand.

Kelsey looked over and saw Ryan, Nicky, Barb, and Ashley. They'd saved a pair of seats for Caitie and Kelsey, but Kelsey barely noticed.

All she saw was how close Ryan and Ashley were sitting. And the little grin on Ash's face that said it all.

"Damn," she cursed under her breath and then sighed. "Story of my life."

"What?" Caitie called, over the noise of the crowd.

"Nothing," Kelsey said, and shook her head.

No sooner had they reached their seats than the

lights dimmed, the curtain was drawn, and the five maniacs who made up Greek Tragedy thrashed into a song that had Kelsey smiling and bopping along in no time.

The hell with Ryan, she thought about halfway through the third song. *I can do better.*

As the fifth song began, Kelsey slipped away to go to the bathroom. She shouldered her way through the gyrating kids until she finally made it to the long hall where the bathrooms were.

The line to the ladies room was brutal. There were at least a dozen girls waiting.

"Oh, great," she muttered. "I'm not meeting Mr. Right if I wet my pants."

"Probably true," said a male voice.

Kelsey turned, eyes wide, and stared up into the face of a guy she'd never seen before. Her cheeks flushed red with embarrassment and she tried not to laugh.

"Sorry," the guy said, also doing his polite best not to laugh. "Couldn't help overhearing. Y'know, if you need to go that bad, there's another john. It's supposed to be for employees, but people always use it at these shows."

Now she perked up. She really did have to go. "Really? Where is it?"

The guy smiled kindly. "End of the hall. Before the door to the kitchen is one marked Emergency Exit Only. Through that, and down the stairs."

Still slightly embarrassed, Kelsey tossed her strand of red hair off her face and grinned sheepishly.

"Thanks," she said. "When I get back, I'll buy you a beer."

"I'll take you up on that," the guy said.

Kelsey followed her savior's directions and pushed through the door, hoping that no alarms would go off, before starting down the stairs. The noise from the bar was really loud—the sound of stomping feet on old floorboards filled the stairwell. It wasn't very well lit, but she started down anyway, her bladder commanding her to continue.

At the bottom of the stairs, she looked around, mystified. She saw only a metal door, which obviously led outside, and a small wooden door set into a crooked frame. *This building really is ancient.* In the half-light, she moved over to the small door, thinking if there were rats inside, well, her bladder would just have to wait.

She grabbed the knob and gave it a twist. It stuck at first, but she put a little weight behind it and it squeaked open. It was dark inside, and Kelsey reached in and felt around for a light switch. She found it, and snapped the light on. It flickered to life, and for a moment, she just stared.

It was a storage closet. Mop, bucket, that sort of thing—and it was the only room down here.

"Oh, man," she said angrily. "What a jerk."

Then she let out a small yelp as a powerful hand clamped over her mouth, and she was yanked violently back against the chest of the man standing behind her.

"Now is that nice?" the man asked amiably and drew a scalpel across her throat, severing her carotid artery and her larynx.

He held her so that the spurting blood wouldn't spray him as she struggled and tried to scream. With her larynx cut, she could make only the most pitiful sounds. Nothing would be heard upstairs. Eventually, she fell limp against him, and he laid her down. With the scalpel, he cut away her clothes.

He told himself there was nothing improper in that—he had to do it, after all, to expose her chest. Quickly, he removed the tools from the inside pockets of his coat. Then he set about his work.

It was no simple task, removing a human heart.

chapter 1

"Come on, Jenna, live dangerously."

Jenna Blake raised an eyebrow suspiciously at the chunk of raw fish that dangled in front of her face on the end of a small fork. *Sushi*. Even the word disgusted her.

"Melody, that is so nasty," Jenna said, shuddering.

With a shake of her head and a mischievous grin, Melody LaChance popped the piece into her mouth, chewed a bit, and swallowed.

"Jenna, darlin'," she said, her southern accent more pronounced than usual, "ya'll have to broaden your horizons."

"Oh, right," Jenna replied with a sardonic chuckle. "Says the girl who has Captain Crunch for breakfast every single day."

Melody blinked, embarrassed, and then shrugged. "You know what they say. If it ain't broke . . ."

9

"You could at least try Crunch *Berries*," Jenna prodded. "They're still in the Crunch family, right? But it'd be something different—"

"Don't push me, Blake," Melody said, squinting to look intimidating.

Jenna laughed. "I'm glad you didn't have rehearsal tonight," she said.

Although Jenna loved musicals, she had always been too self-conscious to audition for one. So she was both proud and envious that her best friend had the lead role of Maria Von Trapp in Somerset University's fall production of *The Sound of Music*.

"Even though the show's in two weeks, the director, Alicia, thought we needed a night off," Melody explained. "I think it's more likely that *Miss Alicia* needed the night off, but who am I to complain?"

"Who are *you*?" Jenna asked, fluttering her eyelashes. "Why, Melody, you're the *star!*"

Melody blinked and narrowed her eyes again. "You're mocking me, girl."

"Yup," Jenna said, nodding enthusiastically.

Melody thrust another piece of sushi at Jenna, and Jenna backed up so fast she nearly toppled over. Melody laughed, and it was Jenna's turn to shoot her a withering glance.

"Be nice, or the sushi monster will get you," Melody said.

Jenna rolled her eyes and tried to erase the thought of sushi from her head with a bite of her Hibachi chicken. Their waiter came over to see if everything was satisfactory—which it was. After he walked off, Jenna glanced out the window at the bright lights and the odd collection of humanity that thronged Harvard Square.

She loved it here. *Here* meaning so many different things. Miyamoto's Japanese Steak House—which was famous for its sushi bar—had fast become one of her favorite restaurants. But she didn't just mean Miyamoto's. She meant all of it: the vibrant life of Harvard Square; Boston, only a couple of T stops south of Cambridge; and Somerset University, two T stops north.

Jenna had been pretty fortunate as a kid. Although her parents were divorced, her mom, April, was a surgeon, so they'd never had to worry about money. They weren't rich, but Jenna usually got what she wanted from Santa on Christmas morning.

But she had never really been on her own before she went to college. She'd been to places around the world most kids never get to see, but she hadn't really been out in the world and made meaningful contacts until she got to Somerset.

She knew how good she had it. A great school, a great mom, a new relationship with her father— Frank Logan was a professor at Somerset, so he and Jenna were just starting to get to know each other— and then there were her friends. Jenna took college seriously and spent a lot of time studying. Much of the time when she wasn't studying she was working at Somerset Medical Center. But in what she very sarcastically referred to as her "copious free time," she hung out with Melody, Mel's brother Hunter, and with Yoshiko Kitsuta, her roommate.

Yeah, she was lucky all right.

In the few dark times she did have, waking in the middle of the night or walking along a poorly lit campus pathway, Jenna would feel fear surge up within her again. She was easily startled, what Hunter LaChance called "twitchy." On the other hand she consoled herself with the knowledge that she was getting better—not quite as twitchy anymore.

It wasn't as though she didn't have reason to be twitchy—not after what she'd been through. In the first two weeks of school, Jenna had gotten involved in a genuine mystery, a series of deaths that turned out to be politically motivated assassinations. In fact, she was so wrapped up in it that she had become a target herself, and was nearly killed on two separate occasions. Even her father had been injured, shot in the shoulder, and now, a few weeks later, he was still sore.

The one good thing that had come out of all that insanity, though, was her job. Jenna was a diener, or pathology assistant, for Dr. Walter Slikowski, the county medical examiner, who worked out of Somerset Medical Center. She had always been interested in medicine, but the sight of blood and the thought that lives could depend on her made her very nervous, so her father had suggested she work with patients who were already dead. It was funny at the time, but now Jenna couldn't be happier.

Plus, it was a great compromise for her parents. Her mother wanted her to be a doctor, of course. But her father, a criminology professor, had always urged her toward his field, which was only natural. Truth be told, Jenna really did enjoy the forensic aspects of pathology. Every corpse was a mystery to her, a puzzle, and there was something about that that she really found fascinating.

Jenna loved puzzles.

Of course, all her friends thought working with the dead was completely revolting. And, when she thought about it, there was something about grossing them out that appealed to her as well. She liked being different—to a point. Unfortunately, she'd also found out that working around dead bodies was not exactly turning her into a guy magnet. There was one guy, Damon Harris, whom she'd gone out with a few times. He lived on the same floor in Sparrow Hall that Jenna did. But there was no real spark between them, and they were just friends now.

Other than Damon, she hadn't had much luck meeting guys—or, at least, guys who were interested in her. The one guy she actually had a little crush on was a local homicide detective named Danny Mariano, and he was thirteen years older than Jenna, which was a no-no as far as she was concerned.

Which brought her back to Melody and how

grateful she was to have a friend she could really kick back with and be herself. It was so effortless to be with Melody, to just hang out. They might talk nonstop or just sit quietly. Jenna had never had a sister, but she imagined that it was supposed to be like this.

As if she were reading Jenna's mind, Melody looked over at her and smiled. Jenna grinned back, then glanced around the restaurant. It was busy, but not completely packed. Probably because it was a late hour for dinner, after nine o'clock.

She swallowed another piece of Hibachi chicken and realized that she was stuffed. With a sigh, she pushed back from the table and picked up her glass of watered-down Coke. She swirled the remaining ice in the glass as she sipped from the thin straw.

Melody drank ginger ale, which Jenna thought was disgusting. Why anyone would want to imbibe something that tasted like rusty rainwater was beyond her.

"Done?" Melody asked.

"Totally."

"But you still have room for chocolate chip ice cream from Herrell's, right?"

"Of course," Jenna replied, staring at her friend as though the question were absurd.

Which it was.

A short time later they were wandering through the Square toward Herrell's Ice Cream while Jenna babbled on about the aesthetic value of a chocolate-covered waffle cone, when she heard the muffled thump of music.

"Wonder where that's coming from."

Melody stopped to listen and raised her eyebrows in recognition. "Delgado's," she said confidently. "I think Greek Tragedy is playing there tonight. They're not bad."

Jenna shrugged. "Never heard of them."

"Hunter loves them, if that means anything," Melody explained. "And, hey, speaking of my little brother, where is he? Did he have an excuse for blowing us off?"

Jenna pulled open the door to Herrell's and held it for Melody.

"Not really," she explained, her mind going back to Hunter's casual dismissal of their plans for the evening. "He just said he had some things to do, and that was that. Actually, I've got to say, he's been acting kind of weird lately."

Jenna moved toward the counter, eyes drifting toward the menu. It was relatively late, so the place was almost empty. Just a grungy-looking couple at the counter placing an order, and two older, well-dressed men at a small table. When Jenna realized that Melody wasn't right behind her, she stopped and turned.

Melody was staring at her with a tiny grin on her face.

"What?" Jenna asked.

"You're amazing."

Jenna's expression was half smile and half frown. "What?" she demanded again.

"Hunter," Melody said. "You know he has a total crush on you."

"Oh, please," Jenna said, turning back toward the menu. "I thought he was over that."

"That's what you want to think," Melody informed her. "But you know he's into you. And he did make a sort of snarky remark about how much time we've been spending together. I think he's jealous."

Jenna grimaced at that. She liked Hunter, she really did. She met him even before she met Melody, and they'd hit it off right away. Hunter La-Chance was a sweet guy with boyish good looks and a genuine kindness about him. He was a good listener, which Jenna decided was a talent rare among the male gender, but he was so completely not Jenna's type. There wasn't even the remotest hint of a spark there. She didn't want Hunter to take a romantic interest in her, because she didn't want him to be hurt. In fact, she'd tried to discourage him as much as possible, without telling him there wasn't a chance in hell.

She continued to think about Hunter as the two of them ordered their ice cream—both got waffle cones. Jenna couldn't help feeling a little bad about not returning Hunter's feelings. But then a thought struck her.

"Okay, so he's jealous," she said. "But is he jealous of you, because he likes me and you're with me all the time, or jealous of me, because he hasn't been able to spend as much time with his big sister as he'd like? You guys are pretty close."

Melody thought about that for a few seconds. Then she shrugged.

"Maybe both."

It was quarter past nine when Yoshiko Kitsuta returned to Sparrow Hall. She'd been visiting her friend Rochelle Hamlin down hill. They were in Colonial American History together and had been brainstorming topics for a term paper that was due before Thanksgiving. They had plenty of time, but decided it'd be easier to get started and hit the library if they each had someone urging them on. The buddy system, Rochelle called it. Yoshiko was all for it.

I would never have started this early without Rochelle.

Sparrow Hall was split down the middle between guys and girls. Half of every floor was male, and half female. Each floor had a common area in the center where some studying, too much partying, and the battle of the sexes went on, day after day.

Yoshiko trotted up the north stairs, on the girls' side, to the third floor. When she pushed through the stairwell door, the halls were pretty calm. It was a Wednesday night, late enough so that most people were either in their rooms studying or off doing something that was too early to return from.

The latter would include Jenna, Yoshiko knew. Her roomie was out with Melody, which meant she'd have the room to herself for a bit. Fine with her. She could relax, maybe call home. Send some e-mails. Yoshiko and Jenna were good friends, which was nice, particularly since she'd heard so many horror stories about other kids' roommates.

But they weren't best friends, and that was okay, too. They could hang out together, and they each liked each other's friends, but they had different interests and friends of their own. Yoshiko thought it worked best that way. They lived together, and if they spent every waking moment together, she figured they'd grow sick of each other pretty quick.

So, yeah, it was cool.

Still, she hadn't hung out with Jenna in almost a week. If Jenna wasn't working, she was out with Melody or sitting in on one of Melody's rehearsals, wishing she had had the guts to audition. Then when Jenna was home, she was studying.

Maybe, Yoshiko thought, *it's time to schedule a roomie night.*

She was halfway down the hall when she spotted a lone figure sitting in a chair in the common area. A small smile played across her face, and she took a breath. It was Hunter, who was reading a book, oblivious to everything around him.

As usual, Yoshiko thought. Hunter was pretty oblivious, especially when it came to her. Yoshiko was pretty outgoing. She dressed well—made a point of it, in fact, because it made her happy. She was, in general, pretty confident, but she'd never had a real boyfriend, and so she tended to clam up when it came to one-on-one conversations with boys who might be potential boyfriends. Especially Hunter.

Hunter was something else to Yoshiko.

She had grown up in Hawaii, on the island of Oahu, and the boys back home had pretty much treated her like a sister. Or, worse, one of the guys. Hunter was cute, respectful, had the bluest eyes, and . . . he liked Jenna.

With a sigh, Yoshiko walked past her room, 311, to the common area. She plopped down in a big, ugly brown chair, and held her backpack on her lap.

"Hey," she finally said.

Hunter looked up. When he saw her, he smiled warmly. Yoshiko's heart did a little flip.

"Hi. What are you doing back? Didn't you go to the Square with Mel and Jenna?"

Yoshiko shook her head. "I'm a slave to my studies."

Hunter held up the book he'd been reading. *Things Fall Apart*, by Chinua Achebe. "Me, too."

There was an awkward moment of silence. Hunter and Yoshiko were friends, but their friendship was pretty much defined by the larger group that included Jenna and Melody. When Yoshiko started to get up from her chair, ready to go to her room, Hunter stopped her.

"Hey," he said. "I think I've had enough of being a responsible student for tonight." He took a quick glance at his watch. "This senior, Bill Sheehan, is doing his stand-up act at the campus center at ten. Do you want to go?"

Yoshiko's eyes widened, but only for a moment. Then she grinned, and was happy to see that Hunter grinned back.

"Let me just dump my stuff, get cleaned up a little, and I'll meet you back here in ten minutes," she told him.

"Cool," Hunter said, nodding. "Ten minutes."

Yoshiko hurried back to her room. She dumped her bag, then set about washing her face in the sink, putting on makeup and changing her clothes, all at lightning speed.

Just as she was slipping into a pair of Candies that were a little daring for her, there was a knock at the door.

"I'm coming," she said, smiling broadly. It wasn't really a date, she knew. But it sort of felt like one, and that was a start.

Tossing her shoulder-length black hair back, she pulled the door open, expecting to see Hunter waiting for her in the hall.

It wasn't Hunter.

Norm Crandall yanked open the door to the basement inside Delgado's, and swore under his breath. The music was still slamming into his brain—he'd had a bitch of a headache all night—and now some idiot college punk had puked his guts up right in front of the stage.

The scene that had followed, with the kids spreading out and forming a circle so nobody would step in the vomit, had been enough to bring a smile to Norm's face. But now he was scowling again.

He didn't mind mopping up beer. Didn't mind washing the floor, righting the chairs, cleaning up a broken glass now and then. None of that bothered him. But puke was puke.

Norm stomped down the ancient wooden stairs to the basement, his mind wandering angrily back to the room upstairs. It wasn't until he was three or four steps from the bottom that he blinked in the dim light and realized that he wasn't alone. There was somebody lying on the floor down there.

With a loud curse, Norm shouted at the girl—for he could see long hair and assumed it had to be a girl—to get her ass up and out of there. When she didn't move, his mind finally made the leap. He started to fear the worst. That maybe she'd gotten drunk, gone through the wrong door, and fallen down the stairs or something. Something bad.

He knew it was something bad.

Especially when he finally reached the bottom of the stairs, and the sole of his shoe slid as if he'd stepped in a patch of oil. He looked down at the dark stain on the ground, and he knew. The stain was almost black in the dim light, but he knew.

"Oh, hell," Norm Crandall said weakly, sadly.

"Poor kid," he added, as he reached out to touch the shoulder of the girl.

Her back was to him, and she was so still. He gave her shoulder a little tug, and the body sort of spilled over onto its back. And Norman saw the gaping hole torn in her chest, the jutting bone, and the horrible emptiness where there should have been . . . something.

But there was nothing.

Cursing, he turned and started to stumble up the stairs toward the pounding music above. Norm Crandall almost threw up.

The only thing that stopped him was knowing who would have to clean it up.

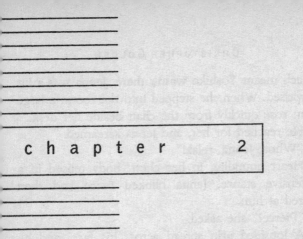

chapter 2

Shortly after ten-thirty, Jenna returned to her dorm. She had walked Melody back to Whitney House, and then continued on up the hill to Sparrow. She used her key at the front door, then took the north-side stairs up to the third floor.

Jenna was tired, but she knew she should spend a little time reading the assignment on the collapse of the Soviet Union for her international relations class. No way would she have missed hanging with Melody tonight, but she didn't want to fall behind, either.

When she stopped in front of her door, Jenna stretched a bit and yawned. She pulled her keys out again—she kept them on a coiled piece of stretchy plastic wire in her pocket—and opened the door.

The only light was from the lamp on her desk,

which meant Yoshiko wasn't there. Jenna was a bit surprised. When she stepped into the room, a large man rose quickly from the chair beside her desk.

He reached for her, and Jenna screamed.

"Whoa, Jenna, relax!"

Heart pounding in her chest, body tensed in a defensive stance, Jenna blinked twice and then stared at him.

"Pierce?" she asked.

A lopsided grin spread across his face, and he scratched his stubbly chin.

"You recognized me," Pierce said happily.

Furious, Jenna punched him in the chest. Pierce didn't even seem to notice, but why would he? He was big and broad shouldered, "built like a Mack truck," Jenna's mother would have said.

"You son of a bitch!" she snapped. "You scared the hell out of me!"

Pierce's grin faltered. He shrugged. "I'm sorry," he said. "I didn't . . . I mean, I caught your roommate on her way out, and she said it would be all right if I waited."

"Yeah, well, she's too trusting," Jenna grumbled. Already her adrenaline rush was starting to subside, and she began to realize how really happy she was to see him.

When she noticed that her puzzle toys and brain teasers were spread out on her desk—Pierce had kept himself entertained while waiting for her—Jenna allowed herself just a faint smile.

"It's good to see you," she confessed. "Even if you did give me total cardiac arrest."

Pierce moved to her and held his arms out wide for an embrace. Jenna moved into them and they hugged. It was awkward. They didn't actually know each other that well, and it had been five or six years since they'd seen each other.

But family was family.

"It's great to see you, too," he said sincerely, still holding her. "And Somerset. Attagirl. I'm proud of you, little sister."

Jenna smiled, and they separated. "I'm proud of you, too, Lieutenant Logan," she told him. "It's hard to believe that you're an officer. The marines must be desperate."

Pierce glared at her, trying to conceal his grin, and then in a flash, he threw her over his shoulder. Jenna screamed as he lowered her to the ground and then set about mercilessly tickling her until she thought she was going to throw up.

When she warned him that he was going to make her barf, Pierce's response was a deep laugh. Then he said, "That's what big brothers are for."

Finally Pierce relented and let her up. For a moment she just stared at him—his dark hair had been scythed into an alarmingly short crew cut. His face was tanned, his jaw square and stuck out at a proud angle. Pierce was still young, twenty-six or seven, but he had the bearing of a much older man.

Where their father was always a bit sloppy, Pierce

was immaculate. Even in street clothes, like the blue jeans and thick white sweater he wore now, he looked like a military man. She suspected that he could make overalls look like a uniform. It was something in his bearing—in everything about him.

Jenna chuckled to herself. He might have terrified her at first, but it was an unexpected pleasure to see her brother.

"So, *jarhead*," she said, and he scowled at the insult, "how long are you in town?"

"I accumulated thirty days of leave, and my C.O. pretty much ordered me to take it. I thought about spending a few weeks in Mexico, but there's just too much trouble to get into down there. So I figured I'd come home for a while, instead."

"Have you seen Dad yet?"

"Of course I have," Pierce replied. "I spent the afternoon with him. He told me where to find you."

"Oh," she said. "I just figured, your being in counterintelligence and all, that you'd be able to figure out where I was."

"I could have," he agreed. "But I'm off duty. No snooping on my own time."

Jenna rolled her eyes and then they began to talk. All thoughts of the schoolwork she had to do, or of getting a decent night's rest, flew out the window. They had so much to catch up on.

Pierce was Frank Logan's son from a failed first marriage. When Jenna's father divorced his first wife, Pierce went to live with her. Later, during high school, he lived with their father, who by then was divorced from Jenna's mom and pretty much out of Jenna's life. She and her brother had never lived together and had never known each other that well, but it had become important to them to communicate over the years. They had no other siblings. So she and Pierce exchanged letters and cards half a dozen times a year. But he hadn't mentioned anything about his visit. That's what surprises were all about, he told her.

Technically, he was her half brother, but Jenna always felt a bond with him, even from a distance. When she was very young, she had adored him as only a little sister can, despite, or perhaps because of, the rarity with which they saw each other. In recent years, however, they had not done a great deal to cultivate their relationship, and it saddened her a bit.

But he's here now, she thought. It was Jenna's chance to get to know Pierce as an adult. As a peer. After all, she wasn't a kid anymore.

They talked forever. About their father, their mothers, Jenna's senior year, Pierce's time overseas, and, of course, about Somerset. When Yoshiko finally came back, at about one o'clock in the morning, Jenna walked Pierce down to the main door, and they talked for another twenty minutes before he finally ended the conversation and set off for their father's apartment, where he was staying.

Jenna watched him disappear onto the darkened

campus grounds, and she smiled broadly. It was so easy to forget that she had a brother. But now he was here, big as life. Thirty days' leave. She couldn't imagine having that much time to kick around. She had always had some kind of job on summer break, so she hadn't had that much free time since seventh grade.

Guilt began to creep over her as she thought about the work she had neglected because of Pierce's surprise visit. She had only written the introduction to her term paper on Rasputin for Europe to 1815, and it was due at the beginning of November. It made her wonder how much of a distraction from classwork her brother might be.

Jenna rolled her eyes. *As if I need a reason to procrastinate,* she thought as she went back down the hall and up the stairs. Yoshiko was asleep when she let herself into the room. Jenna washed up quickly and climbed into bed, stretching as she pulled up the covers.

She was asleep almost instantly.

The next morning Jenna, as usual, was a bit behind schedule. By the time she came back from showering, Yoshiko had already applied what little makeup she wore and was brushing her hair out to a silky black sheen. Still sleepy, despite the shower, Jenna half stumbled into her clothes, and put on a little eyeliner and a lip pencil, which she liked a lot. *I look almost human.* While she was brushing her hair, Yoshiko slipped on her jacket and went to the door.

"Are we having lunch later?" Yoshiko asked.

Jenna blinked. It hadn't occurred to her until just now, but they hadn't talked all morning. She had chalked it up to her own exhaustion, but when she looked at Yoshiko, she thought her roommate seemed troubled.

"Yeah. That'd be great. Morrissey Hall. Also, I'm having dinner tonight with my dad and Pierce. Do you want to come?"

"Hmm. Oh, hey, your brother's really nice, by the way."

"Yeah. He's cool. It's just so weird to see him. All my real memories of him are from when I was a kid. So . . . dinner?"

"Thanks, but I think I'm going to hang on campus," Yoshiko said. "I've got a lot to do. Plus, Hunter said he thought it would be all right if I sat through the rehearsal of *Sound of Music*. I'm interested."

"Yeah, we know," Jenna said with a smirk.

Yoshiko's features grew stormy. Her thin lips formed a tight straight line.

"That's not funny," she told Jenna. "I like him, okay? A lot. And I am going to rehearsal to see him and to see Melody—but mainly just because I find the process interesting. You've been down there half a dozen times, probably wishing you were onstage.

I don't know why you're giving me a hard time about it."

Yoshiko stared at her a moment longer, then reached for the doorknob. Jenna walked to the door and put a hand on Yoshiko's shoulder.

"Yoshiko?" she asked.

When Yoshiko turned to look at her, Jenna was struck by how annoyed she seemed. It was so unlike Yoshiko, and Jenna felt as if she had done something terrible, but didn't know what.

So she asked.

"What?" Jenna demanded. "You're obviously angry with me. Tell me why."

Yoshiko's eyes widened for a second, and then she smiled gently.

"I'm not mad at you, J. It's just . . . it's Hunter, y'know? We had a great time last night, hung out a lot, and barely once talked about you, which for Hunter is sort of a miracle."

Jenna blinked. Frowned. "Wow," she said. "I didn't know it was that bad."

"When I got back here last night, Hunter was just sort of moping around. That's why we ended up going out together."

"He was invited," Jenna protested, but knew instantly it was the wrong thing to say.

Yoshiko sighed. "He's got a mad crush on you. It just isn't pretty."

"And you have a thing for him, which makes it worse, and weird, and awkward, and now it's starting to take a toll on the whole you/me thing," Jenna said, saying what was on both their minds. "I'm sorry, Yoshiko. I don't know what to do about it. How do I talk to him about any of this without either embarrassing him or leading him on?"

That made Yoshiko think. She blinked several times, then glanced around the room. After a moment she looked at her watch.

"I don't know," she said to Jenna. "What I do know is I'm late for class."

"Is Hunter meeting us for lunch?" Jenna asked.

"Maybe," Yoshiko said, shrugging. "I'll see you."

"Yeah."

Then Yoshiko was gone, and Jenna was hurrying to finish getting ready. She put on small gold hoop earrings and some funky brown shoes she'd picked up in the Square. She had to work later and tried to dress pretty conservatively there. But she always wore interesting footwear.

On her way out, she pulled the door shut behind her and then slipped into her jacket while hurrying down the stairs. Her mind wasn't on school, though. Or on work.

It was on Hunter.

She felt bad, but she didn't have any idea what she could say to him. Or if she should say anything. She had to talk to Melody about it, but wouldn't be able to do that until much later.

Continuity of American Lit was fairly interesting that morning. They were studying Jack London, whose work Jenna got into. She had an essay due before Thanksgiving, and she was thinking about writing about nature in London's works. *Kind of a broad topic, though. I'll have to narrow it down some.* Fortunately, she had her own copy of *The Sea Wolf* at school with her, and most everything else London had written was in her bedroom at home.

When class let out at eleven, she headed over to the library. It was built into the side of the hill, so that the front door was at ground level, but if you went up the outside stairs beside the library, you could step right up onto the roof. It was a cool place to study, or just hang out, and it had a killer view of the Boston skyline. Jenna sat on the roof with pen and paper and tried to work on an outline for the rest of her Rasputin paper. She didn't have much time. Her history class was at twelve-thirty, and she had promised to meet Yoshiko at quarter to twelve at Morrissey Hall.

Hunter showed up for lunch, and Jenna was relieved that things were pretty much as usual. Nothing out of the ordinary. Hunter made silly jokes, keeping Jenna and Yoshiko entertained, and the girls rolled their eyes and teased him. Everything seemed fine.

A couple of times, though, she noticed the way that Yoshiko would look at Hunter. And she saw that Hunter hadn't noticed. It made her sad.

*   *   *

Europe to 1815 ended at two, and it was just after two-thirty when she hurried across Carpenter Street and onto the path that led past Somerset Medical School to the Medical Center beyond. She took the elevator up to two and then walked down the hall to the administrative wing where the medical examiner, Dr. Walter Slikowski, had his office.

When Jenna opened the door and slipped in, there was no sign of anyone. The two cubicles in the outer office—one for her and one for the pathology resident, Dr. Albert Dyson—were empty. So was the inner office, where Dr. Slikowski usually only went to check his messages, sort his mail, and listen to frenetic jazz. As chief of pathology for the Somerset Medical Center, as well as county medical examiner and a forensics consultant for local and state police, he was usually only around when there was an autopsy to be performed. And that kept him in the basement.

"Slick," as certain people called the M.E. behind his back, was an in-demand kind of guy. Jenna wished he would spend more time around the office. He was a bit distant, almost aloof, but he was a truly kind man, and his intellect was inspiring. Plus, she had to admit, *his taste in jazz is sort of infectious.*

Although some of her friends had a difficult time understanding it, Jenna Blake loved her job. She liked the science. The medicine. She liked her colleagues. More than anything, though, she liked piecing together the facts of an autopsy in order to offer some kind of peace to the deceased's family and friends. Sometimes, the mysteries were more than puzzles—sometimes there were real challenges.

It was a fascinating job.

Jenna stood alone in the office, taking it all in for a moment. When the phone rang, she strode over to her cubicle and answered it.

"Medical Examiner's office," she said. "This is Jenna."

"Hey. It's Dyson."

"Hey."

"We're about to start down here. You want to help out, or are you pushing papers today?"

Jenna looked at the different reports and documents that needed to be filed, entered into the computer, or transcribed—a few hours' work. She could assist for part of the autopsy, and then come back up.

"I'll be down in a few," she told Dyson. "You want coffee?"

"Please," he replied. "And tea for Dr. Slikowski, if you don't mind. You're gonna love this one, Jenna."

Jenna's mouth twisted in a grimace. "Yeah?" she asked doubtfully. "Why's that?"

"It's a weird one."

Dyson was right, of course. It was a weird one. And while "love it" might have been too strong, Jenna was intrigued by the corpse of the young woman lying on the metal table in the autopsy room.

She'd hit the Au Bon Pain in the lobby of the Medical Center before taking the elevator down to the basement. It was always kind of creepy down there. Not that it wasn't well lit—in fact, the lights were almost too bright—but there were so few people it always seemed a little surreal. There were more administrative offices down here, including facility management and accounting. But at the south end of the corridor, there were just the morgue and the autopsy room. Jenna had only been inside the morgue twice, and she had no desire to spend a great deal of time there.

That was their place. It belonged to the dead.

The autopsy room was different. That was where the work happened, investigating the circumstances of death. In fact, it didn't feel spooky at all to her— as long as she wasn't there alone.

When she pushed into the room, a steaming cup in each hand, Dyson was running a hand through his curly black hair, and Dr. Slikowski was sitting in his wheelchair in the far corner, arranging his tools. Dyson glanced over at her and a welcoming smile spread across his olive-skinned features. His gaze flicked down a moment, then he nodded in approval.

"Nice shoes," he said.

Jenna shook her head. Laughed. It seemed odd to her that a thirty-something pathologist would notice her shoes. But she appreciated the compliment just the same. "Thanks."

At the sound of her voice, Dr. Slikowski raised his head. When his eyes focused on her, he brightened.

"Oh, hello, Jenna. Glad you're here. This is one for the books, I'll tell you."

"Can't wait," Jenna said dryly.

Her humor was lost on Slick, but then, most humor was. He was a thin man, with graying hair and wire-rimmed glasses, and he was on the uphill climb to forty-five. But there was an air of propriety about him that made him seem much older, as though he'd grown up in another era. Jenna appreciated him for his eccentricities—and for his giving her this opportunity over older students. She was getting started very early on her road to medical school, which was good. This she could put on her résumé. Working at the local video store wasn't going to help her any.

There was a sheet covering the corpse. Slick had a sense of decency when it came to the dead. He preferred that they only be uncovered when necessary. Which, for the most part, suited Jenna just fine.

"So what've we got?" she asked.

That was when Dyson said, "Look at this," and whipped back the sheet like an artist unveiling his masterpiece. But this wasn't art. It was horrible.

Jenna's eyes widened. She held her breath a moment and just stared.

"God," she whispered. "What could do something like that?"

Staring at the dead girl, Jenna had made a strange leap in logic. She assumed, at least for a moment, that what had happened to her had been some kind of tragic accident.

Dr. Slikowski disabused her of that notion quickly. He glanced up at her and frowned.

"Don't you mean 'who'? This young woman was murdered in Harvard Square last night, in a club called Delgado's."

His words chilled her. Delgado's. Greek Tragedy had been playing. She and Melody had been close enough to hear the music, and sometime during the night, some vicious bastard had done this.

"It's repulsive," she said simply.

"Isn't it, though?" Dyson echoed, not expecting an answer.

Jenna moved closer to the body. It looked as if the autopsy had already begun, only conducted by some incompetent savage of a doctor. From groin to sternum, the girl's belly had been cut open in a jagged line, and the skin and muscle peeled back to expose the organs. It looked as though some of the organs had been removed and then dumped back into the chest cavity.

But there was more. The girl's throat had been cut, and the edges of the wound stuck out, curling up the way wallpaper does when it gets old and brittle. The corpse had been cleaned, but blood was still encrusted at the edges of the massive incision. The lower bones of the rib cage had been shattered—a few others cracked. It was as though someone had taken a crowbar to her chest.

Then Jenna noticed the worst thing.

Since starting this job, she had been through enough autopsies, even weighing and cataloging organs herself, to realize that something was missing.

She squinted and moved a step closer to peer into the open chest of the dead girl.

"Did they—" she began.

"Yup," Dyson replied before she could even finish her question. "The guy ripped her heart out."

Jenna glanced up at him, frowning. For a moment she wasn't certain if he was making some kind of sick joke about men breaking women's hearts. But then she saw the look on his face and realized he was just as repelled as she was.

Slick wheeled his chair over to the autopsy table. He got in close and worked the controls that moved the table down to give him easier access. Dyson clicked on the tape recorder above them, and Dr. Slikowski scowled as he peered into the open wound.

"Subject, Kelsey Annette Zarin," he began, giving a name to the dead girl.

That made it worse. Knowing the name always made it worse.

"Age twenty," the M.E. continued, examining the girl's body quickly. "Time of death somewhere between eight and ten P.M. Contusions around the mouth and cheeks indicate a powerful grip, probably made by the killer attempting to keep her silent. The throat has been cut, severing the carotid artery and other blood vessels. It would seem to indicate that blood loss is the cause of death, but we'll confirm that as we go."

For a moment Jenna was so distracted by the image of murder that rose in her mind that she didn't compute what he was saying. Then she studied him closely.

"You don't think she was still alive when he . . . did that? Took her heart?"

Dr. Slikowski looked at her. "It's not impossible," he said. "But if it makes you feel any better, she was certainly not conscious at the time."

"Yeah, great," Jenna said.

"Could we get down to work now?" Slick asked.

Jenna winced. He was annoyed that she was focusing on the girl's death rather than the business at hand. It wasn't professional. She didn't blame him, but she also couldn't help herself. This girl was only two years older than Jenna; she'd been killed in Harvard Square when Jenna had been there, not far away. It could easily have been her.

It was too close to home.

She looked back down at the wound. Cut and torn open, her body invaded, violated in the most obscene way. There was only a single word on Jenna's mind. It found its way to her lips.

"Why?" she asked out loud.

"Hmm?" Slick mumbled, opening the massive wound even more to give clear access to the entire chest cavity.

Jenna realized it was her cue. She moved around the table, pulling gloves on quickly, and then reached inside the girl's chest to begin removing the organs as the M.E. started to make his cuts.

"She was already dead, right? Why would he take her heart out?" she asked, more to herself than to the doctors.

"A souvenir?" Slick suggested. "There are many stories, most apocryphal but some true, about serial killers keeping trophies from their victims. Which isn't to say that's what we're dealing with here. Serial killers are actually quite rare, despite what pop culture would have you believe."

Jenna paid little attention to that last part. She was stuck back on what he'd said just before it.

"You mean he *kept* it?" she asked, holding the girl's lungs in her hands. "Her heart?"

"It wasn't found at the crime scene," Dyson told her.

Jenna suddenly felt very cold inside. She went over to the scale to weigh the girl's lungs, but her mind had already left the room. She was numb.

Then something changed. Instead of cold, she was burning up. Instead of numb, she was enraged.

It wasn't just a puzzle. It wasn't just a mystery.

It was an obscenity.

As she looked down at the glazed eyes of the dead girl on that cold steel table, she was filled, suddenly, with the certainty that it wasn't over.

Someone who could do something like this wasn't going to stop after one.

chapter 3

That night Jenna met her father and Pierce at their dad's new apartment. It was only a couple of blocks from where he lived previously; his old building had been burned out the month before. The new place was bigger and more elegant—he had the first floor of an old Victorian that had been completely restored—but it had the disadvantage of being across campus from Shayna Emerson's new place.

Oddly enough, the distance between them might turn out to be a good thing. Shayna was an English professor who'd also lived in the burned-out building. Almost died there, too. Jenna had always liked her and never understood why her dad never asked the woman out. Frank and Shayna had been friends, but after the fire, and the realization that they wouldn't be seeing each other every day, something between them clicked. They'd had three official dates in the past two weeks—Jenna was hopeful.

That night, though, she wasn't thinking about her father and Shayna. In fact, Jenna had trouble focusing on anything because she was still troubled by the autopsy she had assisted at earlier.

At dinner Jenna ignored her father's concerned questions, and instead directed the conversation toward her half brother. Pierce was filled with enthusiasm about the Marine Corps, which was interesting enough to keep her mind from wandering back to the autopsy room too often.

But it did keep coming back to her, haunting her. Jenna tried to stay as focused as possible on dinner and her family. They might be the products of her father's two failed marriages, but they were still family.

Frank Logan was a wonderful man, but solitary. He immersed himself in his work—both the classes he instructed and the research and theory papers he wrote for various journals, which he hoped to compile into a book someday. Just from the exposure she'd had to her dad since arriving at Somerset—they'd seen each other more in the past month than in the previous five years—Jenna could see how his dedication to work might be hard to live with, but she could forgive him that.

What she hadn't forgiven was seeing her father only once a year. Still, she was trying to start their relationship fresh, and so far she was enjoying having her father around.

And now her brother.

It was like constructing a family out of thin air. Which was nice, in and of itself, but one of the problems with family, as far as Jenna was concerned, was that most of the time they felt they had the right—hell, even the obligation—to stick their noses where they didn't belong. Like now, for instance.

Pierce put a piece of swordfish in his mouth. Jenna's father took that as a cue to zero in on her.

"You've been awfully quiet," Frank said, closely studying his daughter. "Is everything all right?"

Jenna had a bite of swordfish halfway to her mouth, but paused when her father spoke. *He just doesn't get it.* She'd been sending the don't-ask-don't-tell signal for an hour, but he just couldn't grasp it.

"I'm fine, Dad," she said. "Really. Just had a long day, and beyond that, I'd rather not discuss it."

Though she'd spoken amiably enough, her father frowned. He looked a bit put off.

"Well, excuse me," Frank replied. "Just a bit of paternal anxiety. It sort of goes with the territory."

Jenna couldn't help it—she rolled her eyes. "Isn't it a bit late to start with paternal anxiety now?" she asked. "I mean, it hasn't exactly plagued you before."

She didn't know what to expect, but she was unprepared for the hurt that crossed her father's face. Her words were harsh, but she knew that wasn't the only cause for his reaction. No, his pain was there because her words were true.

"Dad, I'm sorry," she said, waving her fingers in front of her face, brushing the whole thing away. "I've just . . . it's been a terrible day."

"That's all right," he said, nodding slowly. Then he shrugged. "Something's bothering you, but it is your business, and I shouldn't have pushed. If you want to talk, you know where I live."

Jenna offered a small smile of relief, and her father did the same.

Pierce just shook his head. "Wow," he said, "you guys are rough. Remind me not to get into the family tag team thing. And don't ever try to ambush me on a talk show."

"Not unless you dress in drag," Jenna replied with a smirk.

"Hey, mind your own business," her brother said. "Just be glad your clothes wouldn't fit me."

Once again Jenna rolled her eyes, but this time she was laughing. She caught her father's gaze, and their eyes held—they were okay. That was important to her. They didn't have much of a relationship before, but they were building one now, and though she couldn't forget past disappointments, she wasn't going to let old recriminations get in the way.

"So, before you were so rudely interrupted, you were talking about Camp Pendleton," Jenna prompted.

Pierce nodded enthusiastically, and Jenna finally ate her bite of swordfish.

"It's just north of San Diego," he said. "The greatest weather in the world, I swear to God. I guess the only place I'd rather be stationed is Hawaii, and that may come around as well. You really should come visit—both of you. I work long days, but I can manage a little time."

"It wasn't all that long ago you were thinking about leaving the Corps," Frank interrupted. "Not that I want to have an argument with both my children on the same day, but what happened? You know I'm not the biggest cheerleader for the military. I was glad you were looking at the FBI, DEA, and ATF. They'd all jump at someone with your training and references."

Pierce took a deep breath. Jenna studied the stormy expression on his face but didn't know what to make of it. Finally her brother shook his head.

"No, I'm sticking with the Corps. It won't be long until I make captain, and who knows where I can go from there. I'm in one of the best counter-intel units in the nation. I can't walk away from that."

"Right. Counterintelligence. Which would be the opposite of smart, right?" Jenna teased.

"Very funny," Pierce replied. "There are people who want information they're not supposed to have, and it's my job to see that they don't get it."

Jenna narrowed her eyes. Pierce's job was fascinating, even though it was about keeping secrets, and hers was about uncovering them.

"So what kind of things do they teach you?" she asked.

"Well, aside from the usual, we have intensive instruction on observation, surveillance, intrusion, and countermeasures for all three," he told her.

"Wow," Jenna replied. Then something occurred to her. "When you learn hand-to-hand combat, is there a particular martial art they focus on, or—"

"No." Pierce waved the question away. "They teach you how to fight. How to figure out what will work in any combat situation. They also train marines to use bayonets, and, one of the most interesting things . . . we have these things called puguil sticks, which are sort of like fighting staffs with pads on the end. They train us to use our rifles as blunt weapons, for close-quarters combat if we run out of ammunition—"

"So they teach you to kill," their father said over the rim of his coffee cup. "How original."

"Dad," Pierce replied. That was all he said, but it was enough.

"I know," Frank added. "It's the job."

"I don't get it."

Danny Mariano looked over at his partner, Audrey Gaines, and offered her a small shrug. "What's not to get?" he asked.

"Kim. What happened to the two of you? What did you do?"

Audrey was driving with both hands on the wheel. She was a very cautious driver, but she managed to shoot him a sidelong glance.

"What do you mean, What did I do? I didn't do anything. We only went out four or five times. She doesn't want to go out anymore. What am I supposed to say?" Danny protested.

Audrey kept her eyes on the road as Danny took a long swig from the bottle of Coke in his hand. They'd gotten the call about seven minutes earlier. Homicide. 322 Winthrop Street. They were rolling on it now, and, of course, Audrey had picked this time to start talking about their personal lives.

"Y'know, you haven't had a date since . . . what, March? You shouldn't talk," he told her.

"Don't change the topic," Audrey chided. "We're talking about you. I'm not the one who got dumped."

"You can't call it dumped when we only went out six times."

"I thought you said four or five."

"Whatever!" Danny snapped, exasperated.

"Do you think she met someone?"

Audrey's tone changed for that last question—it was quieter, calmer. She cared. He knew that much; had always known it. They were partners, and they were friends. Audrey was less than ten years older than he was, but she'd taught him almost everything he knew about being a detective. She was very good at the job, but when it came to people skills, she didn't have much going on. It had taken them a while to get close.

"Look, I just . . . it sucks, okay?" Danny said, exasperated. "I had to cancel a couple of times. Tuesday, we were working on the Gittleman case. I didn't call. She was worried, and then she was pissed, and then . . . she said that she was just sad. She doesn't want to be with a cop. This kind of life isn't for everyone, y'know?"

Audrey nodded slowly. "I know," she said.

She did know. Their choice of occupation was hard on family and friends, but worse on lovers and spouses. Danny suspected it was half the reason Audrey had never married and rarely dated. He also knew she still hoped.

"Hey," he said, "let's give it another couple of years. Then, if we're both still single—"

"We'll shoot each other," Audrey finished for him.

Danny laughed. Shook his head. "Not what I was going to say," he told her, "but you're on."

Then their time for banter was over, and Audrey was now steering their unmarked car up the long driveway of the beautiful faded green Victorian on Winthrop Street. There were two prowl cars in the drive and an ambulance out front. The ambulance wouldn't be needed, of course. Nor would the paramedics it carried. Soon enough, the crime scene unit would arrive and start taking pictures and dusting for prints, all of the minutiae that goes into investigating a homicide.

The front door gaped like an exit wound. The house had been transformed into apartments sometime in the past decade, and several of the tenants were on the front lawn, giving statements to cops in uniform. Danny and Audrey got out of the car and made their way to the house, where Claire Bellamy was guarding the door.

"Hey, Sarge," Audrey said as they approached.

Sergeant Bellamy nodded her greeting, letting her eyes flick back and forth between them. "Detectives," she said.

"What've we got?" Danny asked.

"The victim is Anthony Soares. Lived alone on the second floor. Retired. The first-floor tenant, a Mrs. Haskell, heard noise from his apartment last night, about ten o'clock, she says."

"She didn't call it in?" Audrey asked.

"Soares was in his late sixties, apparently partially deaf. Always had the TV blaring. Mrs. Haskell figured that's what it was. That's what got her to thinking, by the way. The victim apparently watched *Wheel of Fortune* every night at seven. But last night no *Wheel of Fortune*. He had the Fox channel on. When she knocked to check on him, there was no answer, so she called us."

"Quite the detective, our Mrs. Haskell," Danny observed.

"You can interview her when we're done up-stairs," Audrey said.

They moved past the sergeant and into the foyer of the building. Danny had already crossed to the stairs when Sergeant Bellamy called in to them.

"Just wanted to warn you," the woman said. "It's a mess up there. I don't know if you heard about the one in Cambridge night before last, but this is like that."

Heard of it? Danny thought. Of course they'd heard of it. Suddenly he wasn't in much of a hurry to get upstairs, and he knew Audrey wouldn't be either.

At the top of the stairs they passed a uniformed patrolman by the name of McKeown. Danny said hello, and McKeown barely nodded. He was pale; in fact, he looked as if he might be ill.

"In the kitchen," McKeown mumbled as Audrey passed him.

Danny paused at the door.

"You coming?" Audrey asked from inside.

"Try and stop me," Danny said. "Please."

There was no stopping now, they both knew. Danny followed Audrey through the living room and into the kitchen. It was warm inside the apart-ment and the corpse had begun to smell. Danny put the handkerchief that he carried solely for that purpose over his face.

Whenever anybody noticed it and asked about it,

51

he lied. Let them chalk it up to eccentricity. Cops didn't ask—they knew.

The smell was awful. And it wasn't just the dead man. It was the blood. So much blood. They had to stop about three feet into the kitchen to avoid stepping in it. At least until the crime scene unit photographed everything.

From where they stood, they could see the old man's ruined body, his insides splayed open, his heart ripped from his chest.

"Oh, God," Danny muttered through the cloth over his face.

"Yeah," Audrey agreed, covering her own mouth. "And this is number two. We've got to catch this guy, before he does it again."

Alan Carstairs, the crime scene photographer, had stepped in behind them, but Danny didn't realize he was there until the man spoke up.

"What makes you so sure he'll do it again?" Carstairs asked.

The guy was new to the job, which was obvious from his question, and the way he carefully avoided looking at the dead man.

"Look around," Danny replied. "This guy is having way too much fun."

On Friday Jenna arranged for everybody to meet at Espresso's for pizza. She'd pretty much blown her friends off the day before, and now she wanted them to know why. It was after one when she and Pierce walked in to find Yoshiko and Hunter sitting at the one round table big enough for five.

Espresso's did most of its business in takeout and delivery, and it was kind of small.

"Hey!" Jenna said happily as she and Pierce pulled up chairs. "You guys have already met, but let's make it official."

Hunter, who sort of puffed himself up in Pierce's presence—*typical male macho weirdness*, Jenna thought—reached out to shake.

"It's a pleasure to meet you, Pierce," he said. "Hunter LaChance."

"Good to meet you, too, Hunter," Pierce replied. "Jenna speaks highly of you."

Jenna blinked. Hunter was her friend, but she hadn't exactly bragged about him to her brother. When Pierce paid him the compliment, Hunter brightened visibly. She chewed her lip a moment, then offered Hunter a small smile when he glanced at her for confirmation. *Great! Pierce just made my little problem that much worse.*

"Good to see you again, Yoshiko," Pierce said.

Jenna's roommate smiled. "You, too. I've got to tell you, Jenna told me she had a brother in the military, but I figured you'd be Mr. Mystery for the next four years. It's nice to have you around."

"I had a lot of leave saved up," Pierce said. "And it's a beautiful time of year in New England. I'll be here right through Halloween, which is my favorite holiday."

Hunter grinned. "You know, there's a tradition that the residents of Sparrow Hall run naked around the quad every Halloween at midnight."

"Yeah. Not this resident," Jenna said.

"Trick or treat," Pierce replied, with a small chuckle.

Yoshiko rolled her eyes. "Men are all dogs."

"You can say that again," said a familiar voice.

Jenna turned to watch Melody pull up a chair. She looked amazing, as usual. Her burgundy shirt looked as if she might have stolen it from an old boyfriend, and her hiphuggers appeared to have been cut just for her. Her long blond hair tumbled across her shoulders, and her makeup was flawless, as always. Not an extra line or spot of blush.

It was just Melody. Casual clothes, relaxed makeup, hair blown dry. And the final product was always perfect. Jenna reminded herself to ask Mel how she did it—and then break her nose.

"Hey," Jenna said warmly.

"Sorry I'm late," Melody replied.

"We just got here," Pierce told her. Then he put out his hand, "I'm Pierce. And you can only be Melody."

It was something in his voice. Jenna heard it right away; she wondered if the others heard it as well. Pierce had been smitten with her the minute he looked at her. Not that Jenna could blame him, and not that she'd complain. Mel was her best friend, and Pierce was her brother, and a good guy to boot. But Melody had pretty much sworn off boyfriends for the semester. She was a sophomore, and her second semester freshman year had been kind of disappointing academically, so she was committed to making up for it now, so . . . no boys.

Melody held her hand out to take Pierce's, and she smiled at him. As Jenna watched, astounded, Melody actually glanced away shyly like the proper southern belle and coquette she most certainly was not.

"That's me," she said. "And a pleasure to make your acquaintance, Pierce."

Hunter actually laughed at his sister. He must have found it as amazing as Jenna did to see her, well . . . flirting.

"All right, Scarlett, just relax," Hunter said.

Yoshiko and Jenna both laughed, and Melody even chuckled a little. When she turned away from Pierce, she was back with a vengeance all of a sudden. Her smile turned to a sneer, and she shot her brother a withering glance.

"See you in hell, Hunter," she said pleasantly.

"You're my big sister," he replied. "I grew up in hell."

Then the moment passed, but it wasn't the only one. As they ate and talked, Pierce and Melody had plenty of opportunity to speak by themselves. There was definitely some serious chemistry happening, and Jenna didn't quite know what to make of it.

Later, when Pierce got up to hit the men's room, Melody leaned over to Jenna. "You never told me he was such a babe."

"He's twenty-seven," Jenna replied, grinning. "I didn't think you'd care."

Melody shook her head and then laughed, mostly at herself, Jenna thought.

"I feel so awkward," she said. "I'm never like this. I'm usually much more at ease with these things. I like a guy, I get his attention, and maybe he asks me or I ask him out. Pierce probably thinks I'm an airhead, now."

"I don't think so," Jenna said.

She might have elaborated, but then Pierce came back, and the conversation turned to more mundane things.

"So, Jenna, did I hear right? Your I.R. class is canceled today?" Yoshiko asked.

"Yeah. The professor is apparently sick with a stomach virus or something."

"Wow. A free afternoon," Hunter observed. Then he glanced from Jenna to Pierce and back. "What are you guys going to do?"

"Work," Jenna said. "Dr. Slikowski asked me to go into Cambridge and pick up some crime scene reports on a murder case we did the autopsy on yesterday."

"You're kidding," Hunter said. "With e-mail and fax machines, you've got to go pick up a document?"

"The medical examiner's office requires the official reports. That means documents with original signatures. I'm faster than the post office, and cheaper than a messenger," Jenna explained.

"So what is it? The heart thing?" Melody asked, making what Jenna had come to think of as her "*eew* face."

"Yeah. The heart thing," Jenna admitted. She didn't like to think about it either. "Anyway, I've got to get going after we eat. When I get the documents, I'm supposed to work the rest of the day."

"You want to hit a flick tonight?" Yoshiko asked.

"That'd be cool," Hunter chimed in.

Jenna glanced at Pierce, who was busy looking at Melody. "Well," she said, "Pierce and I are going to the gym to work out at seven. But if you wanted to hit the late show . . ."

"Sounds good," Melody said.

Now Pierce spoke up, "Yeah. I'm up for it."

Jenna raised an eyebrow. "I'll bet you are," she said.

Both Pierce and Melody smiled, embarrassed. Jenna realized they had all just arranged her brother's first unofficial date with her best friend. If anything came of it, she figured, she could get used to the idea. But she was also worried that if they did start hanging out and things went badly, it could make the rest of Pierce's stay kind of uncomfortable.

Then again, that's their business.

And, after all, in a world where somebody could rip another human being's heart out for entertainment, there were worse things than romance.

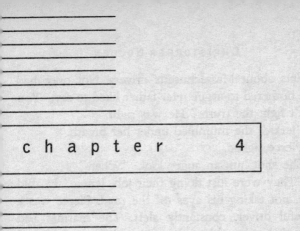

I can't believe those jerks," Jenna grumbled as she flipped through the police reports on her lap.

Pierce kept his eyes on the road. The traffic coming back from Cambridge was crazy as usual, and even worse when it came to the sudden splits and one-ways and rotaries. Jenna hated rotaries. Roundabouts, Melody called them. Didn't matter what you called them, though, the little traffic circles were hazardous because nobody paid any attention to the law. People already in the rotary had the right of way over anyone trying to get in, but cars were always shooting in from one of the four or five different streets that fed into the circle, and to hell with stop or yield signs.

Since she'd come to Somerset and met so many people from out of state, she heard constant complaints about Massachusetts drivers. Not once had she bothered to argue. Her father liked to say, "You can't fight the truth." He was right.

"Jerks," she mumbled under her breath.

Pierce sighed.

She shot him an angry look. "What?"

"They were just doing their job, Jenna," he told her, not taking his eyes off the road. Pierce was a careful driver, constantly alert. The marines had drilled that into him.

"It's *embarrassing*," she protested. "They call up my boss to check on me? That guy said I looked like I was in high school."

"Until a few months ago, you *were* in high school," Pierce reasoned. "You are sort of young to do the job you do."

"Okay, but what was he thinking? I told him where I was coming from, what the case was, everything. Pierce, I assisted in that autopsy. That guy just had an attitude."

"So did you," he told her gently. "Crazy as it sounds, it's possible some reporter could have paid you to go in and ask for those reports. Those guys are doing their jobs, just like you. Following orders. Policy is policy."

Now Jenna rolled her eyes. "Spoken like a true marine," she said. "And if the Corps told you to jump off the Tobin Bridge?"

Pierce's eyes narrowed and his jaw clenched. For the first time, he tore his eyes from the road and turned to glare at her. "I don't think I like your tone, little sister," Pierce said angrily.

Jenna dropped her gaze, then looked out the window. They were on University Boulevard now, passing by Somerset—almost to the medical center.

"Yeah, well, now you know how I feel," Jenna replied.

They were quiet after that. After Pierce drove around the back of Somerset Medical Center to the visitors' parking area, Jenna stepped out of the car. She was about to shut the door without saying anything, but then thought better of it.

"Hey, Pierce, I'm sorry," Jenna said, leaning back into the car. "You know I meant no disrespect."

Pierce's features softened. "I know," he told her. "And you're right; those cops didn't have to be so dismissive."

Jenna smiled. "I'll see you at quarter to seven? Then, if you're still mad, you can whup my ass in the gym."

Pierce had suggested they work out together while he was in town and offered to show her some self-defense techniques. Jenna figured it would be fun and give her a bit of self-confidence if she could defend herself better. She'd taken a course in high school, but after being assaulted the first week at Somerset, she decided that it hadn't helped her that much.

"You think I need permission to whup your ass?" Pierce asked.

"Just you wait, buddy. You are *so* in trouble."

Her brother laughed. Jenna shut the door and then turned to hurry into the Medical Center, the police reports in a manila envelope clutched to her chest.

When she reached Dr. Slikowski's second-floor office, she found a note in Dyson's handwriting in her cubicle.

Jenna, it read. *Got another one.*

For just a moment butterflies fluttered in her stomach. *Flutter-bys,* she thought. That was what Winnie-the-Pooh called them. Dyson hadn't been specific, but he wouldn't have written "another one" in reference to a random autopsy. She understood what he meant and had no desire to see another corpse with its heart torn out.

But that was the job. She'd seen some pretty horrid things since she started working as a pathology assistant—once, Dyson had even thrown up—but Jenna had handled it all pretty well. For some reason, though, the violence of this case, the violation of human life, had gotten to her.

Still, she had to go down and assist. Dyson wouldn't have left the note if they weren't expecting her. Jenna shrugged out of her jacket, then walked into Slick's office and left the police reports on his desk. On her way down, she stopped at the coffee shop and got herself a cappuccino. Then she got back on the elevator and rode it down to the basement.

As she walked down the corridor, she took a sip of her cappuccino. When she lowered the cup, she noticed two people at the end of the hall outside the autopsy room. She recognized them immediately. Somerset's finest. Audrey Gaines and Danny Mariano.

A small smile tugged at the edges of Jenna's mouth. Seeing Danny did that to her.

Okay, he's thirty-one, but a crush is a crush.

"Hello, detectives," Jenna said as she approached.

"Jenna, hi there," Detective Gaines said.

She was a generally grumpy woman, but Jenna had managed to get on her good side somehow. Audrey Gaines knew her father, and that had apparently helped. Not that she really cared what Detective Gaines thought of her.

Detective Mariano, on the other hand . . .

"Hey, Jenna," Danny said, nodding at her cappuccino, "I don't suppose you brought enough for everyone?"

Jenna blinked. "Um, no," she said. "Sorry. I didn't know you guys would be here, and, um . . ."

"He's teasing," Audrey said blandly, barely glancing at Jenna.

Danny chuckled, and Jenna narrowed her eyes at him.

"Now I'm not even going to offer you a sip," Jenna said in a petulant little-girl tone.

"Be that way," Detective Mariano replied.

"So, don't you two have anything better to do

besides hang out with corpses all day?" Jenna asked, focusing on Danny.

"Not really," Danny lied. "Pretty pathetic, when you think about it. What about you? Surely there's something an attractive young college girl can do to occupy herself that doesn't involve dead people."

Jenna raised her eyebrows at that, and thought she might even be blushing a little. *Attractive young college girl?*

Danny'd just crossed the line from banter to flirtation, and Jenna liked it. A lot. She had to remind herself that he was probably still just teasing. He was much older than she was, after all. *I mean, okay, Pierce is eight years older than Melody, but this is . . . I mean, Danny's like thirteen years older than me. He's in his thirties. Still . . .*

"Nah," she replied a bit nervously. "I guess we're stuck with each other."

"I can think of worse things," Danny said.

Jenna tried to fight the smile that was taking over her face because she knew she must look like a crazy person or something.

"Like what's in that room, for instance," he added, his manner suddenly becoming grave.

Her mind flashed back to the autopsy she had worked on the day before, the savagery of the murder, and all the pleasure of their flirtation left her. She wondered if he sensed he'd gone too far, and purposely changed the subject. That was what they ought to have been talking about after all. Death. Homicide.

"It's pretty nasty," Jenna agreed.

"I thought you just got here," Audrey said, after shooting Danny her disapproval.

"I did," Jenna replied. "I'm talking about yesterday. The one from Cambridge. There was something so . . . disturbing about it."

"Yeah, as soon as Slick gives us some feedback, we're headed over to Cambridge to talk to the detectives on the victim they had over there," Danny said.

"I just got back from there," Jenna told them. "The police reports are upstairs. I'm sure Dr. Slikowski would let you take a look at them."

"Thanks, but we need to talk to them in person anyway."

Audrey raised an eyebrow. "He sent you over, huh? Some face time with some of the other local departments. That couldn't hurt in the long run, establishing relationships."

Jenna rolled her eyes. "Oh, please. Those guys were so, like, go-away-little-girl. Barely gave me the time of day."

Then, quite purposely, she met Danny's eyes. "They aren't anywhere near as friendly as Somerset cops. I'd rather have you guys coming to my rescue any day."

Now it was Danny's turn to chuckle nervously. Jenna felt her stomach flip again, but not because of the autopsy. This time, it was because she couldn't believe she'd just said what she'd said. Or, more precisely, said it the way she'd said it. *Talk about out-and-out flirtation.*

She covered her embarrassment by taking a long sip from her cappuccino, then added, "I guess I should go in."

"Better you than me," Danny replied.

"See ya," Jenna said idly, trying to act cool as she pushed through the door and into the autopsy room. When the door had closed behind her, she slapped her forehead with an open palm. "Idiot," she muttered under her breath.

"Jenna, just in time," Dyson said. "Looks like our heart thief is back."

She saw Dr. Slikowski adjusting his wire-rimmed glasses as he examined the open chest cavity of this second victim. Dyson held the dead man's liver in his hands.

"Great," Jenna said and crossed the room to scrub up.

In life, the corpse had been an older man, probably Latino. Probably with family, friends, maybe children. She'd had similar thoughts about the family and friends of the girl who had been killed in Harvard Square two nights earlier.

There were people out there who were grieving now. People who wanted and needed answers. Dr. Slikowski would study the dead man. Based on how the man's blood had settled, how his body had stiffened, he would determine when the man had died, and in what position he'd been lying. With Dyson's help, he'd remove organs and fluids. With Jenna's help, Dyson would weigh them and label them for the lab. Eventually, the body would be released back to the deceased's next of kin, back to those who grieved for him.

The dead man had a hole in his chest where his heart had once been. They all knew how he had died, but they'd go through the motions and do the job, because sometimes things weren't what they seemed. Slick had told Jenna that several times in the first week. What looked like a car accident could just as easily be a poisoning. What seemed to be murder might instead turn out to be nothing more than a fatal misstep and bad fall. Sometimes the hardest question had the simplest answer, but usually the truth was more complex.

The medical examiner's job was to find that truth. Jenna wanted to be a part of that.

This had to stop.

It was almost six o'clock by the time Jenna got back to Sparrow Hall. She was running a little behind, so she just warmed up some soup on the hot plate in her room. While it was heating, she peeled off her work clothes and dumped them in her laundry basket. They smelled of formaldehyde, as they always did when she assisted with an autopsy. Dyson and Slick had promised her she'd get used to the smell and the way it burned her nostrils. It hadn't happened yet, but she was still hopeful. Yoshiko had recently complained about the smell, so Jenna cracked the window a bit, hoping the fresh air would help. A chilly October breeze swept in, and she shivered, then rushed to pull on her workout clothes.

She was psyched about working out with Pierce because Jenna had heard enough horror stories about the notorious "freshman fifteen," the extra pounds that freshmen often put on. Anxiety and bad nutrition were a deadly combination, and Jenna experienced plenty of both. And she'd been slacking off on exercising ever since she got to Somerset.

With sitting in class for hours, sitting and studying or surfing the Internet in her room, and sitting at a computer terminal at work, the most exercise she normally got was assisting in an autopsy. All of which appalled her. She'd been trying for the past week or two to get back into regular workouts. Time on a treadmill, or just a jog—that would be enough. She had decided to ask her mom to bring her bike up, but it was almost winter, and snow and cold would seriously curtail her riding.

There was always early morning swimming at the gym—that would be good. But first she had to make a start. She knew which road was paved with good intentions, and Jenna had no intention of going there.

When her soup was warm enough, she ate it

quickly, then pulled on her hooded Somerset sweatshirt and zipped it.

On the way to the gym, she jogged.

The workout was very cool. After warming up, Pierce began by showing her a series of blocks and throws that would help if she ever had to defend herself. When she asked for some offensive moves, he told her she had to master defense before worrying about offense.

Which was when she told him about the night she'd been assaulted, several weeks earlier.

"Whoa," Pierce said, his brow furrowing. "You never told me about that."

"Trying to forget," she told him. "But I'm also trying to be prepared in case it happens again."

Pierce nodded. "All right. Let's go through the same scenario, for starters. We're still on defense, though, which should be enough to begin with."

Despite her discomfort at reliving the events of that night, Jenna was appreciative. The new moves that Pierce showed her would be easy to remember and seemed to be effective in breaking away from an attacker.

"And, of course," Pierce said, getting up from the mat where she'd dumped him, "if none of that works, you can always kick him between the legs. Clean shot in the tenders will stop any guy cold for a bit."

"Are we going to practice that one?"

"I don't think so," her brother replied, one eyebrow raised.

Jenna grinned mischievously. Pierce showed her another throw, and then they hit the stationary bikes. Later, working with a weight machine, Jenna was amazed at Pierce's strength. She didn't want big, defined muscles, but watching him lift, she decided it wouldn't be bad to be a bit more muscular, a bit stronger.

It was after eight when they decided to wrap it up. Despite her bragging, she was going to have a lot of bruises the next day.

"You'll make a marine out of me yet," she said, her voice pained.

"Don't flatter yourself," Pierce replied, and laughed.

Jenna hit him, and that set them off again wrestling for a few minutes. When Jenna saw the clock on the wall, she swore loudly and nearly shoved Pierce toward the men's showers. She took a quick shower herself and changed.

Much to her surprise, she was ready before Pierce. When he came out, he looked bright and clean and neat. She wasn't sure, but she suspected that he had shaved. His bristly crew cut stood at attention and his clothes were as immaculate as usual. She marveled again at how different he was from their father, who was always rumpled.

"We should hurry," he said.

"Yeah," Jenna agreed. "You don't want to keep Melody waiting."

"Or Hunter."

Jenna rounded on him. "Oh, man, not you, too!" she cried. "For the last time, nothing's happening there. He's totally not my type."

Pierce nodded. "Great. But try telling him that. That boy's got it bad. Trust me, I've seen that look in the mirror too many times. Guys know."

In the car Jenna turned the situation over and over in her mind. Hunter was a good guy. He liked her, but Jenna wasn't interested. And, of course, to make things worse, Yoshiko . . .

"Ah, hell," she swore to herself.

They were the last ones at the theater. Hunter had bought five tickets for the new Will Smith movie, and Jenna didn't protest. She hadn't seen a movie in more than a month.

"Hey, thanks," Jenna said, taking her ticket from Hunter. "I want to get some popcorn. Anybody else want anything?"

She took a couple of orders. Yoshiko had a Junior Mints addiction—but only ate them at the movies— and Pierce had to have popcorn. She caught Melody's eye, and gave her a wink.

"Why don't you guys go in and get us seats," Jenna said, before turning to Hunter. "You don't mind sticking around to help me carry everything, do you, Hunt?"

The poor guy looked as if she could have

knocked him over with a feather. "Huh?" he grunted. "No, no, not at all. I'd be happy to help."

Jenna smiled thinly. That southern charm. Anybody else would have said, "That's cool." Jenna just hoped she'd say the right thing to Hunter.

But what was the right thing?

The truth.

When Yoshiko, Pierce, and Melody had gone into the theater, she and Hunter stood in line and talked about nothing while waiting to pay for bags of stale popcorn and three-dollar candy bars.

"So, you guys got out of rehearsal early," Jenna said. "Anybody give you a hard time?"

"Actually, rehearsal was only six to eight tonight. No problem at all."

"Good," Jenna said distractedly, and nodded.

After they gathered up all their junk food, Jenna started for the darkened theater. She hadn't said anything. Didn't know if she could. She didn't want to embarrass Hunter—that was the last thing she wanted. But she had to talk to him.

"Can I talk to you about something?" she asked, after the skinny high school kid in the blue blazer had ripped her ticket.

"Sure," Hunter replied, barely balancing his drinks and popcorn.

Jenna stopped and looked into his eyes. "It's kind of personal," she said. "And, well, I'm probably going to sound like a royal bitch, not to mention arrogant."

Hunter blinked. The smile disappeared from his face. He was an intelligent guy, and Jenna had the feeling that he knew what was coming. But now that she had begun, it would be impossible to stop.

"You're a great guy," she said, and immediately regretted it. Those words were the kiss of death, and she knew they both heard the *but* coming. So she changed tactics.

"Am I your friend, Hunter?" Jenna asked, watching him closely.

He hadn't expected that. She could tell. He offered a sort of shrug and then nodded. "Of course you are, Jenna."

"I'm glad," she said. "Because I want that. It's important to me that we're friends when we're old and have grandchildren. I want to be around to be happy for you when you find the person who's just who you want, and I want you to do the same for me. To be happy when I find the person who's just right for me."

Hunter smiled weakly. "I understand."

She leaned forward and kissed his cheek. "I'm glad," she said. "And I also wanted to tell you that, if you keep your eyes open, you might just realize that the person for you is with you now, and you were just looking in the wrong place."

His eyes widened and Hunter looked at her thoughtfully. Jenna started for the theater, where the coming attractions were blaring from the flickering darkness.

"Wait," Hunter said behind her. "You mean Yoshiko?"

Jenna was already pushing through the door, goodies clutched in her arms. She didn't bother elaborating. *Let Hunter figure it out himself. I've done my part.* And he seemed to have taken it rather well, all things considered. He really was a sweet kid, but that was the problem—she thought of him as a kid.

Melody and Pierce walked along the path that ran past the library, hand in hand. It was very late—after midnight. They'd gotten to talking at the movies, and after they dropped off their respective carloads, they met back at the Campus Center. It was closed, this late at night, but that was all right. All they really wanted was to walk, and talk.

They talked about the marines and about Pierce's family. What his mother was like, and why she had left his father.

They talked about Louisiana, the LaChance family, and the rambling house on the Mississippi where Melody's mother was slowly drinking herself to death, surrounded by hired help. Her father—who had never been around much—had died several years before. As much as she loved her mother, and the house, thoughts of home had become bittersweet.

"I'm sorry," Pierce told her, his heart going out to this beautiful, intelligent girl.

"Well, your father wasn't around much either," Melody said, tossing her hair to one side.

Pierce nodded. "Right. But he was more the absentminded professor. He was never cold—just the opposite, in fact. He was great to be around, when he was around."

That left them silent for a moment. They stood behind the chapel, the half-moon shining in the cold, clear night.

"Oh, hey, come up here," Melody said, breaking the moment.

Melody dragged Pierce along the path and up to the roof of the library. At the far end, she stopped, and together they leaned on a concrete wall and gazed at the Boston skyline on the horizon.

"Wow," Pierce said. "This is an extraordinary view. I didn't know you could see Boston from here. It's like a postcard."

"Yeah. Romantic, isn't it?"

Something in her voice made Pierce turn. He looked into her eyes, and smiled.

They were quiet for a long moment.

"I was at a party last week," Melody said, "and the weirdest thing happened."

Pierce was a bit confused by the change of subject, but he nodded to indicate that she should continue.

"I was on the front steps of the Arts House, talking to a guy I've known since the first day of my freshman year. We were in the middle of the conversation, and he was staring at me. I said, 'What?' I thought I might have food on my face or some-

thing. He said, 'Can I do something I've been wanting to do for a long time?' So I said yes, and he
kissed me."

Pierce raised his eyebrows. Melody hadn't said
anything about a boyfriend, but it was certainly possible she had one.

"And?" he asked.

"Nothing," she replied. "That was it. One kiss.
Then we went on with our conversation. He might
ask me out at some point, but I'm not really interested in him. Still, it was a nice kiss."

Pierce stared at her a moment. He didn't know
what to do. This was his little sister's best friend,
after all. He also didn't know if she really was interested in him, if that's where all this was headed.
But there was just something so electric about her.
He smiled softly.

"Well, then," he said, holding her hands and
moving a bit closer to her. "Can I do something
I've been wanting to do for . . . well, at least since
this morning?"

He dipped his face down, tilted it, prepared to
kiss her.

"I'm not sure that's—"

Pierce bit her lightly on the nose.

"Hey!" she said, laughing and whacking him on
the arm.

It was what he'd planned—a way to test the wa-
ters. A little joke between friends, if she didn't re-

spond. But she had responded. She was hesitant but there wasn't a *no* there. Not even close.

Pierce smiled. This time he really did kiss her. It was soft and tender, and lasted only a few seconds. When he pulled back, they smiled at each other again, and Melody rolled her eyes and shook her head.

"This is a little crazy," she said.

Pierce couldn't disagree. "You're worried about what Jenna will think?"

"Aren't you?"

"Not so much. I think she'll be happy. I was more concerned with the fact that I'm eight years older than you, and I'm stationed three thousand miles away."

Melody smiled at that, and Pierce thought he could see the lights of the city in her blue eyes.

"You worry too much," she said.

This time, it was Melody who kissed him, rising up on her toes and pulling his head down to hers. This kiss was a bit longer. And more intense.

When it was over, he took a deep breath, and let it out. "You're something else, you know that?" he asked.

Melody nodded. "Yeah. I know."

It was after one o'clock when Jenna finally went to sleep. She had gotten in from the movies at eleven-thirty, but sat up talking to Hunter and Yoshiko for half an hour. She didn't know if Yoshiko had noticed, but Jenna could tell that Hunter was looking at her roommate a bit differently.

After Yoshiko went to bed, Jenna logged onto the Net. She checked her e-mail, and was happy to see that she had messages from both Moira Kearney and Priya Lahiri, her two best friends from high school. Moira was at USC, and she was excited because it was barely a month into college and already she'd been asked to be on the crew of a student film.

Priya, on the other hand, was not having as good a time. She was at Northwestern, in Evanston, Illinois, and was feeling very depressed and homesick. Jenna spent some time composing replies to both of them, and to the three other messages she had— two of which were jokes sent along from friends on other campuses, and the last of which was a pretty racy and obviously fake picture of Katie Holmes that Damon Harris had sent.

Jenna rolled her eyes at that one.

When she was through with her e-mail, she spent forty-five minutes doing some rather grisly research on "the heart thief." It occurred to Jenna that someone who would do something as savage as this was very likely to have done it before. So she used the Internet to search for similar crimes.

To her disgust, there were many. Killers taking organs, or mutilating their victims' organs. But not one specifically matched this case.

By the time she went to bed, she was even more

haunted by the crimes than when she had begun, and dismayed that she had found no connections. But she wasn't about to give up.

She only hoped she wouldn't have nightmares.

A little after three o'clock in the morning, a nondescript brown Honda Civic moved along University Boulevard, and then took a left up Carpenter Street. The car was on its third circuit of the Somerset University campus, its driver examining as much of the landscape as he could from the car. Plenty of trees, he observed. And the academic buildings would be deserted at night.

The heart thief had found a new hunting ground.

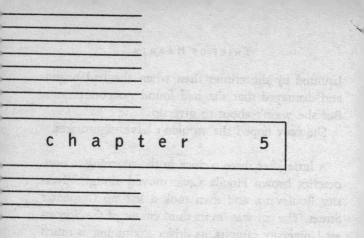

chapter 5

The building that housed the Somerset Police Department was located just outside of Somerset Square. Once upon a time it had been used as city hall. In time, however, it had become home to the city's police force, and a barely adequate home at that.

The small homicide unit was housed on the third floor of the old brick building, and the light was terrible. The one good thing about the building, according to just about every cop who worked there, was that the wiring had been updated only the year before. Finally the computers and phone systems were working the way they were supposed to.

It was little enough, but, as Danny Mariano had said to Audrey Gaines on numerous occasions, it was something. Progress was progress.

On Saturday morning Danny was at his desk before Audrey arrived. That had never happened. Not once since they'd been partnered. It had been quiet the night before, so they were left with very few messes to clean up.

After a minimum of small talk—Audrey was even crankier first thing in the morning than she was during the rest of the day—they set about writing reports on the previous few days' events. But Danny's mind was drifting. As he sat and typed, he looked up frequently. There were four other desks in there, but all of them were empty this morning.

Nobody else was on today, and the lieutenant wouldn't be in until after twelve.

Quiet. Quiet's good.

But the quiet was bothering Danny today, for some reason.

He hadn't even finished his reports before he set them aside. Instead, he reached for the results of the canvass they had conducted the previous afternoon. Uniformed officers had helped out in questioning the residents around the Winthrop Street house where Anthony Soares had been so brutally murdered two nights before.

Their massive effort had come up with absolutely nothing, and forensics had very little. No fingerprints. No clothing fibers. A few hairs that *might* belong to the killer—Mr. Soares didn't have many visitors. *But unless we have a suspect to match those hairs up with, they won't come to anything—*

"You're not writing," Audrey said.

Danny looked up, rolled his eyes, and took a long sip of his black coffee. Audrey tilted her head to one side, studying him closely. There was an over-sized plant on her desk that she fed too often, and Danny was always surprised by that. The idea that Audrey would take the time to nurture anything but a case befuddled him.

"Danny?" she prodded.

"Sorry," he said, and spun in his chair. He looked back at her. "This murder is bothering me."

"Soares."

Danny nodded. "Town like this, we get husbands and boyfriends turning brutal, jealous wives, crack-head parents, the occasional gang shooting or street brawl. That kind of murder is easy, in a way.

"I just don't want to start thinking that's all we can do. That when something comes up that isn't simple, it gets the better of us."

"You know that isn't the case, Danny," Audrey said, frowning. "We've solved clueless murders before."

"Yeah. And there are a handful we haven't solved. In the few years I've been in homicide, a handful is too many," Danny said, meeting Audrey's gaze. "Under normal circumstances, I'd say we pull in every known relative of this guy, try to find someone who squirms too much. But with the Cambridge killing . . ." He let his words trail off.

"It's just the beginning," Audrey said at length.

"I know that's what you're thinking, Danny, and you're right. We've got exactly nothing to help us yet. And he'll be back."

"That's what's eating at me, Audrey," he confessed. "Knowing he'll be back. And probably soon. Two murders in two days. Hell, who knows what he might have been up to *last* night?"

"I'm worried, too," she admitted. "We can't call him a serial killer yet, but at least the FBI profiling unit is working something up."

Danny scowled. "Yeah, and that feeds what I was saying before. Why do we have to turn to someone else every time something out of the ordinary turns up?"

"You know the profiling unit is invaluable. And in the meantime, we should call Slick to see if the lab results are in from the Soares autopsy. Maybe he'll have some news for us," Audrey noted.

With a sigh, Danny leaned back in his chair. "Why don't we take a ride over there instead. Dispatch will give us a shout if anything comes up."

A small, uncommon smile spread across Audrey's features. "You're amazing," she said.

"What?"

"You just want to see your little girlfriend, don't you?"

Danny blinked. He stared at Audrey, pretending, at least for a moment, that he had no idea what she was talking about. But, of course, he knew exactly what she meant.

"Audrey, she's just a kid," he said, shaking his head.

"Right," Audrey agreed. "Just a kid. But a cute, intelligent, courageous kid with whom you were seriously flirting the last time you two ran into each other."

For a moment, Danny was speechless. Then he made a sort of clucking sound with his tongue. "She's eighteen," he told his partner. "I don't even think that's legal."

"Weird? Yeah. Sad? Uh-huh. But illegal? Oh, I don't think so. Come on, Danny. She has a thing for you and you like it, admit it," Audrey teased.

"It isn't . . . she's nice, okay," he said defensively, feeling ridiculous for defending himself at all. "Jenna's all the things you said. But can't I like her and admire her and not be some lecherous old guy lusting after a teenage girl?"

"Oh, lusting now, are we?"

"I didn't say that," he snapped, angry now.

She laughed. "Danny, you're not old. Thirty-one is not old, and if you say it is, I'll have to shoot you. And sure, you can be friends with her, but I'd hate to see her fall in love with you and then get hurt."

Danny only shook his head. "You don't have anything to worry about," he said. "Besides, what makes you think she'd get hurt?"

Audrey looked a little shocked, but Danny only smiled mischievously.

"Anyway," he added, "I don't think she works weekends."

When he stood up to grab his coat, Audrey did the same.

"Good," she said. "Then we're safe—at least for now."

Jenna spent the weekend decompressing. On Saturday, after reading assignments for history and bio, she went shopping in Boston with Yoshiko. Sunday, they mostly hung out. Things were weird between Jenna and Hunter, but not so bad that a little time together as friends wasn't more helpful than hurtful. In fact, when she decided to make chocolate chip cookies in her little toaster oven on Sunday night, pretty much all was forgiven.

At least on the surface.

Yoshiko and Hunter shared several amused glances, and Jenna was hoping they would hit it off. It would ease any remaining guilt she had about disappointing Hunter, but more important, she hoped it would make them both happy.

It seemed to Jenna that too many of her friends felt a kind of sadness about being single that she deemed completely unnecessary. Of course, necessary or not, that didn't save Jenna from the same sadness. It wasn't a constant. Not at all. But it was there, just the same.

Jenna tried to be understanding when Melody and Pierce were both suddenly unavailable over the course of the weekend. So much for Jenna's new workout partner. So much for hanging with her half brother, or her best friend. At least for a couple of days.

Late Sunday night she talked to Melody, and they made plans for dinner Monday. It made Jenna feel a little better, even though she would barely admit to herself that she'd been feeling bad. She wanted Pierce and Melody to be happy. If that meant with each other, that was great. She just hoped they wouldn't abandon her.

Monday morning, as she was getting dressed for class, and a little bit of melancholy still swirled around in her head, she ate the three cookies that had survived the pig-out that she and Hunter and Yoshiko had engaged in the night before.

"That's your breakfast?" Yoshiko asked.

"Why is it worse than a Pop-Tart?" Jenna demanded.

Yoshiko said, "Pop-Tarts have no cholesterol," as if it were an enormous revelation.

"You should be a lawyer," Jenna noted. "You have the flair for it."

Yoshiko tossed her hair back. "Thanks."

"Don't mention it," Jenna mumbled through a mouthful of chocolate chip cookie.

Later that morning, she had trouble paying attention in both biology and Spanish. It didn't help that she was falling behind in Spanish. The whole language thing had never been easy for her, but the professor moved along so quickly that the class was becoming quite difficult. She felt as though she had a faulty circuit somewhere. But Language Arts were part of the core curriculum. No way was she graduating without it. She only hoped it wouldn't damage her freshman year GPA too badly.

After crisscrossing the campus several times, going from class to class to lunch to international relations at the other end of the academic quad, it was a relief when it was time to go to work. It wasn't far off campus, but it felt like leaving Somerset University behind for a few hours.

Working with Dr. Slikowski was an escape for her. While she was only one of a thousand freshmen at Somerset, she was a class of one as a pathology assistant. Plus, she felt as though they needed her—and that was nice.

Even better were the words out of Dyson's mouth the moment she walked into the office Monday afternoon.

"Oh, Jenna, thank God," he said, one hand brushing through his tightly curled black hair.

Jenna blinked. "What? Do we have one on the table?"

Dyson smiled at her use of the jargon. Then he shook his head. "Not now," he said. "And no more from our madman. Dr. Slikowski is in Boston this afternoon. We did have two autopsies over the weekend and one this morning. I haven't had a second to start transcribing or filing."

"No problem," Jenna said. "I'll get right on it."

"You're the best," Dyson told her enthusiastically. He handed her a small stack of files and then gave her a bunch of tapes as well. The folders were piled with the oldest on top and the most recent on the bottom, to keep things running in an orderly fashion. Slick demanded it. When Jenna looked at the top folder, she recognized the name immediately. "Anthony Soares."

"Hey, Dyson," she said, watching him settle back down at his desk.

He turned, chin tilted up inquisitively.

"Please tell me nobody else had their heart ripped out this weekend," she said, dreading going through the pile.

"Nope. A car accident, a suicide, and a fire."

"Oh, goody," Jenna said, aware of the perversity of the relief she felt to hear of such horrid deaths. But compared to the alternative, she'd take suicides and burn victims any day.

"Any progress on catching the guy?" she asked, partially to make conversation and partially because she was still a bit haunted by the first victim, a college girl like herself.

"None at all," Dyson said. "Apparently the Somerset and Cambridge cops are trying desperately to find some connection between the victims. At least that would give them something to work with. But so far, *nada*."

Jenna set about her work.

She didn't like knowing there was a killer running loose out there. But she supposed that knowing was better than not knowing at all.

"So, Jenna, you're sure you're okay with this?"

Melody was so earnest, so serious, that Jenna couldn't help but laugh a little. They had agreed to get Chinese takeout and hang out at Whitney House until Mel had to take off for rehearsal. Melody's roommate was at her boyfriend's, as usual. But when Jenna arrived at the rambling white colonial that had been converted into student housing, she found that Pierce was already there.

They made small talk while they waited for the food to arrive, and then some more small talk while they ate out of little white cartons. When the food was gone, Melody had finally broached the subject they all knew was coming. Pierce sat on the edge of the bed next to Melody and offered Jenna the closest thing to a repentant-little-boy look that a marine lieutenant could muster.

"Guys, you don't need my permission to hang out together," Jenna said, shrugging.

Pierce had pretty much sat by silently while Melody explained that they really liked each other, and that they were worried it might bother Jenna. But now he piped up.

"We know we don't need your permission, but we also know it might be weird for you. And more than that—"

"Look, Sleepless in Somerset, what do you want me to say? I'm okay. It's fine. You try not to make me feel like a third wheel, and I'll try to appreciate being with you and my best friend and ignore the fact that you're sucking face all the time."

Pierce stiffened. "Jenna, that's not—"

"Joke, Pierce," Jenna said, holding up a hand. "Joke."

Melody laughed, then stood up and hugged Jenna. "He's totally not my type, you know," she whispered conspiratorially.

"That's why you like him," Jenna told her.

They both chuckled. Pierce glared at them and shouted, "Now cut that out!"

"Y'know, he's going to be a lot more fun to tease now," Jenna observed.

"Oh, yeah, I'll give you all the dirt," Melody replied.

With a deep breath, Pierce fell back onto Melody's bed. "What have I gotten myself into?" he asked out loud.

"You have no idea," Melody said mysteriously.

Jenna suddenly asked, "Don't you have to get to rehearsal, your diva-ness?"

Melody glanced at the clock and swore loudly. Then she was a dervish, changing her clothes and leaving Pierce and Jenna standing on the front lawn of Whitney House staring after her.

"I notice that she didn't ask you to leave the room while she changed," Jenna said after a bit.

It was getting dark, but she could have sworn Pierce was blushing.

"Okay, people, listen up!"

From the third row of Coleman Auditorium, Melody and Hunter LaChance glanced up to see the show's director, Alicia Davis, waving her right hand in the air to get the cast's attention.

As Maria, Melody had at least half the songs, and the entire show revolved around her.

Hunter had been cast as Rolf, the messenger boy. It wasn't a very large role, but he got to sing one of the show's best numbers, "You Are Sixteen," and dance with Jacqui Forrest, the cute senior girl who was playing Liesl.

Best of all was the fun Melody and Hunter were having doing a show together. The last thing they'd done was *Oklahoma* at their private high school. Melody usually gave her brother a hard time, but she really did love him. When he'd decided to come to Somerset, she couldn't have been happier. In fact, doing this show together had made Melody think that maybe her senior year she'd make a pitch to direct the fall show. Then she could cast Hunter as a lead.

Not only will it be fun, but he'll have to do what I say.

"Guys, please, settle down for a second," Alicia said, exasperated.

Melody gave the director her full attention. The girl was a senior at Somerset and lived on the top floor of Whitney House. Melody had never spoken to her before auditions, though.

"Okay, things went very well tonight," she said. "But I could tell we need to reblock a couple of scenes. I'd like to take a closer look at 'So Long, Farewell,' and 'Maria.' Otherwise, we're in good shape. All of which means—a little drum roll, please—if the rest of the week goes as well, you can have the weekend off.

"Don't forget dress rehearsals are next Monday and Tuesday. So far it looks like we'll have next Wednesday off, so you can rest your voices. And then the curtain goes up a week from Thursday. Any questions?"

Nobody raised a hand.

"Great, go on home. Get some rest."

The chatter started immediately. The cast and crew rose as one, and Melody and Hunter moved off toward the door at stage left. Beyond that was the greenroom where they'd left their jackets and bags.

"Hey, guys," Jacqui Forrest said, catching up with them at the greenroom. "We're going to the Stable to hang out, get something to eat. You want in?"

The Colts' Stable was a local bar and grill owned by Somerset alumni and named after the school's sports teams, all of which were called the Colts. A lot of seniors hung out there, mainly because it was one of the closest places they could legally drink. But the Stable also had some pretty good live music from time to time.

"Can't tonight, Jacqui," Melody said. "Sorry. I have plans."

"Anyone I know?" Jacqui asked, with a conspiratorial grin.

"I doubt it," Hunter chimed in, then looked at Melody. "Are y'all going out, or staying in?"

Melody blushed a bit.

"Staying in," she told him.

"All right, I guess it's the Stable for me," Hunter announced.

He and Jacqui struck up a conversation and Melody thought about how jealous Yoshiko would be if she could have seen Hunter then. She wished the girl would just come out and tell Hunter she liked him, but Melody didn't see much chance of that. *Nope, Hunter will have to learn about women the hard way.*

Some of the other cast members were already drifting out when Melody tapped Hunter on the arm.

"I'll catch up with you tomorrow."

"Sure," he agreed. "And if not, I'll see you at rehearsal tomorrow night."

Then he returned his attention to Jacqui, and Melody shook her head. Poor guy. He actually thought he could hit on a senior girl and get somewhere. Hunter was a freshman but didn't look much older than sixteen. Melody didn't have the heart to tell him that.

She left them there and went out into the stairwell and down to the basement. The halls under the auditorium were lined with rehearsal rooms, and, in one section, with several rows of soundproof rooms, where musicians could practice without disturbing others. The rest of the basement was for storage of costumes and props and set pieces.

And the bathrooms, thank God.

The basement was well lit with sickly fluorescent lighting that made everything look washed out, but even so it was very creepy. The rest rooms in the basement had been installed several decades earlier and hadn't been updated since. They were kind of dingy.

Melody hurried.

Outside, Hunter was thrilled to be flirting with Jacqui Forrest, even if she was merely indulging him. In the musical, they danced together and kissed, and he definitely enjoyed their kiss. But he heard she had a boyfriend, and he hadn't had much luck with girls lately. But Jenna's comment had given him something to think about. Still, he'd have to be brain-dead not to be attracted to Jacqui. She was something else.

They headed for the Campus Center, where Jacqui had apparently parked her car. *It must be a wonderful thing*, he thought, *to have a car on campus*.

Just as he had that thought, Hunter noticed a man in a dark-red raincoat. He was on the other side of the street, walking toward the auditorium and University Boulevard beyond. The streetlight was out, so Hunter didn't get a look at his face. In fact, he wouldn't have noticed the guy at all if it hadn't been for the raincoat.

He looked up. The sky couldn't have been clearer. For just a moment Hunter wondered why anyone would wear a raincoat on a night like this.

Then Jacqui was giggling about something and grabbed hold of his arm. Hunter forgot all about the man in the raincoat.

Back up in the greenroom, Melody slipped on her jacket. She picked up her book bag, which doubled as a purse, and walked down the three steps into the auditorium proper. She looked back at the stage and smiled, feeling the pleasure of being the star. It wasn't arrogance, really, but rather the satisfaction of accomplishment.

Something behind her, some small noise, made her turn to look back up at the main doors. Halfway down the center aisle, moving toward her, was a man in a dark-red raincoat.

"Ah, there you are," he said amiably. "I'm glad I didn't miss you. I was waiting for you outside, but when you didn't come out, I thought I should come in and look for you."

As he spoke, the man continued down the aisle toward her. Melody frowned, hefted her bag farther up on her shoulder, and glanced around to see if anyone else was there.

"I'm sorry, you were waiting for me? Do I know you?" she asked.

By then he was only half a dozen feet away. Her first thought was that he was a reporter, here to do a story about the production. But then she took a closer look at his eyes and the way he smiled, and something clicked inside her. Alarms went off.

Melody took a step back, moving toward the stage.

The man whipped a scalpel out of the pocket of his raincoat. Both frightened and furious, she slipped her heavy bag from her shoulder and swung it at him. The man put a hand up to ward off her blow, but as the bag slammed into his hand and face, he was set off balance for a moment.

Melody ran.

Half a dozen steps to the stage. She leaped up onto the wooden surface, and took off sprinting for the stage-left wings. There were stairs at the back, which she ran down so quickly she nearly fell several times. At the bottom of the steps, she emerged into a short corridor that went under the stage to the far side. Actors could exit by this route on one side of the stage and enter on the other.

But halfway down that little corridor was a door that led out into the basement proper.

Melody slammed her hands against the bar across the door. It popped open and she burst through, heart hammering, breath coming fast and ragged.

Oh my God, she thought. *This just doesn't—*

Her thoughts were interrupted as she spotted the man in the red raincoat at the other end of the hall. *He must have come down the stairs by the greenroom,* she thought frantically. Then she was running again. She had a good lead on him, and though she hadn't seen anyone down there before, she figured that at this time of night there must be somebody around, rehearsing or playing music.

Someone . . .

But there was no one.

Melody had only one hope. There was a central staircase that led up to the first floor at the front of the building. *If I can just reach that,* she thought, *I can get outside.* And once outside, she could scream bloody murder.

Someone'll hear me.

Someone.

Heart slamming against her rib cage, a splinter of pain shooting across her scalp—a major headache coming on—Melody ran full tilt down the corridor.

Then, as if a fog had been cleared from her brain, her ears tuned in to the fact that she heard nothing behind her. No running feet, no rustle of raincoat, no heavy breathing. As the fact of it hit her, she reached the end of the corridor. He wasn't behind her. He was in front of her now, blocking the bottom of the stairs that would take her up and out. Standing there, leaning against the wall, and grinning at her.

Melody screamed. Just stood still for a moment and screamed.

Then he was walking toward her. His arm flew up from his side, the scalpel gleaming in his right hand, and he began to sing.

"How do you solve a problem like Maria?" he crooned. "How do you trap a cloud and pin it down?"

She knew the tune, knew the words, knew the song—it was from *The Sound of Music*. And she was Maria. She was the problem he had to solve.

With barely enough breath left to scream, Melody bolted back the way she had come. But instead of running the length of the corridor, she took her second left, at a T-junction that led to half a dozen of the soundproof music rooms.

It was a dead end, but she hoped he hadn't rounded the corner in time to see her duck down the side corridor. Had to hope, as she slid into one of the soundproof rooms, that he wouldn't hear the gentle click as she closed the door and locked it.

There was a small window, almost like a porthole, in the door, and she glanced out for a few seconds. A few heartbeats. Until she realized she didn't want to see him because that might mean he could see her, too.

So she sat on the floor, back to the door, out of sight of the window, and kept completely silent. She wanted to move the piano up against the door, but didn't dare risk the noise.

For more than two hours, she sat there, moving only when she had to. More than once, Melody found herself holding her breath.

Then, not long before midnight, she let out a long sigh, and stood up. There must be a security guard walking around somewhere. She decided her assailant wouldn't have hung around this long. Plus, she was hungry and tired. *He's gone*, she told herself. *No way would he have hung around down here, when anyone could walk by.* She decided that he had probably checked a few of the rooms or searched back up in the auditorium. By then he would have realized the risk and taken off.

Melody looked out the little window onto an empty hall and shook her head. She'd go home and call the cops right away. *And they'll pick the bastard up, too.* His features would be etched on her mind forever. She'd gotten a very good look at him.

With a grimace, she turned the knob. The door unlocked. She slowly pushed it open and stuck her face out of the music room.

The killer shattered her nose with the first blow. Melody staggered back into the room, too stunned to cry out. And when she had recovered enough to scream, he had already pulled the door shut and locked it. The room was soundproof.

No one would hear her.

She put up a brief fight before he slit her throat, holding her against the piano, her body jerking against the keys and creating a horrible jangling that wasn't music at all.

It was her death song.

Jenna couldn't miss the disappointment on her father's face when he walked into the Campus Center to see her sitting alone at a table by the window.

"Okay," she said as he approached, "maybe breakfast with your one and only daughter isn't the number one thing on your agenda this morning."

Frank smiled and bent over to kiss her head.

"I'm sorry, honey," he said. "I was just hoping Pierce would be here. He didn't come in last night until about three and when I got up this morning, he'd already gone."

Jenna frowned. "I'm missing something," she said. "Didn't he know we were having breakfast?"

Frank slid into his chair and put down his canvas bag. He ran a hand through his tousled hair.

"He knew. But I'm not surprised he didn't come. We haven't spoken since Saturday night."

"What was Saturday night?" Jenna asked, confused.

Frank shrugged. "We had an argument. He's just . . . he's so stubborn. He won't even sit still long enough to listen to logic. It's not like I'm trying to get him to change his life, but I'd appreciate it if he'd at least listen to my opinion. But he doesn't know how."

Jenna blinked a couple of times, waiting for her father to explain. She nodded, urging him to continue. He wasn't getting the message. "Dad? What *happened*?"

Frank sighed. Shook his head. "You have to understand, Jenna. I'm an open-minded guy. But come on, marine counterintelligence is barely half a step down from working for the CIA, for God's sake. The federal government in this country puts on a grand show of democracy, of being 'of the people, for the people, and by the people,' but that's a load of crap."

Jenna leaned back in her chair. "Ooo-kay, Dad, maybe you'd better start at the beginning."

Frank looked at his watch. "Maybe we'd better get some breakfast, and then we'll see if you think I'm as crazy as your brother does. Who knows, maybe you'll talk sense into *one* of us."

Yeah, Jenna thought. *Like I want to get in the middle of this argument. I'm also really lobbying for ritual facial scarring and a shiny new brain tumor.*

"What?" her father asked, looking at her.

"Nothing," she said, rolling her eyes. "Let's eat."

Jenna was constantly trying to convince herself that she enjoyed breakfast. The idea of eating something in the morning didn't bother her as much as the kind of things that were served. Every time she had herself convinced that a Belgian waffle or bacon and eggs or a western omelette was a good idea, she'd get a quarter of the way through the meal and realize that she'd made a mistake.

Bagels were good. Also blueberry muffins. Fruit and yogurt were probably the best, and Pop-Tarts were her secret pleasure. Of all the things people traditionally ate for breakfast, Jenna could usually only truly appreciate French toast or cold cereal. The consistency of oatmeal she found completely repulsive. But Cheerios were a staple of life.

Jenna put a lot of thought into breakfast.

This morning, it was a bagel with cream cheese and a cherry vanilla yogurt with Grape Nuts sprinkled on top.

"Breakfast of champions," she said as the cashier swiped her meal card through the scanner.

The woman grunted and barely looked up. Everyone was so pleasant in the morning.

When she and her father had returned to their table, Jenna tried hard not to look at the mishmash of greasy things on his tray. Instead, she kept her eyes on his face, trying to figure out how his brain worked.

"So, rewind, Dad," she said. "Return with me now to the days of yesteryear."

Frank blinked. "Hey, *Lone Ranger*," he said happily. "You remember watching—"

"Ancient reruns every Saturday morning on Channel 38, right up until you bailed on Mom," Jenna said, without any of her usual bitterness. "I stopped watching it after you left, but I never forgot."

Her father seemed touched by that, and then his face grew dark again. "I've always been a liberal," he said.

"Bleeding heart, I believe Mom called you."

Frank smiled. "Yeah."

"Not that there's anything wrong with that."

"Gee, thanks," he said. "Anyway, I have pretty strong feelings about this country. Which can basically be summed up this way: it's the greatest failed opportunity in the history of mankind. It could be the closest thing to perfect in the world. Instead, our government is all about personal power. Congressmen routinely ignore their constituencies the moment they take office, and then pay lip service to them when an election comes around."

Jenna nodded. She'd heard most of this before, and couldn't completely disagree, although she didn't think things were quite as dismal as her father painted them.

"Still," he said, "I'm a realist. I know things aren't going to change overnight just because they're wrong. I also know that as the most powerful nation in the world, we need to have the best military available. That means soldiers. And the military can have its own rewards. Pierce has earned money, learned extraordinary discipline and respect for others, and developed skills that could very easily be put to use elsewhere."

Finally Jenna understood.

"I get it," she said. "He's been in long enough. He stays any longer, and instead of benefiting from the corrupt government, he becomes a part of it?"

Frank grimaced. "It isn't quite that drastic, Jenna," he said. "I just feel that rather than involving himself in things that are morally questionable and possibly despicable, he could at least consider a position that isn't quite as compromised. DEA. FBI. Even police or private investigations. He could do any of that, with his current training."

"Dad," Jenna said, trying to get him to focus on her. "Maybe Pierce will make that decision at some point. But right now, nothing's more important to him than the Marine Corps, and you have to respect his decision."

Her father was lifting a forkful of hash browns to his mouth when he put the fork down and leaned back in his chair.

"No, Jenna. I'm sorry, but I don't. I have to accept his decision, but I don't have to respect it."

Jenna blinked and shook her head. "No wonder he won't talk to you."

They ate mostly in silence before Jenna excused herself. She had some errands to do before class, she said. She lied. She just wanted to get out of there.

She put her tray away and walked out, book bag over her shoulder, hoping the rest of Pierce's stay wasn't going to be like this.

Maybe his being with Melody is the best thing that could have happened, she thought. *That should keep Pierce and Dad out of each other's hair.*

Jenna loved Tuesdays and Thursdays. In the morning, she had American Lit, which consisted mainly of talking about books, something she'd do even if it weren't for class credit. Then, after lunch, she was held spellbound by the European history lectures of Professor Mark Georges. He was the best teacher she had ever had. Thus far, they'd had only one test, and Jenna had pretty much aced it, and with very little studying.

She didn't need to study. The amazing thing about Professor Georges was this: he opened his notes at twelve-thirty, gave an enthusiastic, amusing, and truly interesting lecture, and always finished precisely at two without ever checking the clock. If one went to class, took notes, and read the assigned materials, all one had to do was read the notes over once or twice to pass his tests.

"How can that be?" Hunter had demanded when Jenna had been bragging about Professor Georges.

"Easy," Jenna said. "He lectures so well that you *remember*. When a question comes up, it's almost like I can picture him explaining it in class. Trust me. If you want to do well in any history course, you should try getting into one of his classes."

By the time she got out of American Lit, Jenna had almost completely forgotten about her father and Pierce. *Let them fight it out,* she'd thought, more than once.

She ate an early lunch at Keates D.H. with some kids from the class who were forming a study group, then went back to her room to get her book bag. They were reading *Billy Budd, Sailor* by Herman Melville in her literature class, and the paperback was all she had needed that morning. *Billy Budd* was turning out to be pretty enjoyable, too. She was thinking about making it one of her essay subjects this semester. Her professor was going to love it: "The Homosexual Love Triangle in Melville's *Billy Budd, Sailor.*"

It wasn't a topic that had come up in class, but she definitely thought it was there. *Original thinking. Ought to earn me an A.*

In her room she saw that the message light was blinking on the answering machine. Three messages: *probably Mom, Dad, maybe Yoshiko wanting to make dinner plans.* Jenna was one of those people who returned calls as soon as possible. Therefore, unless she wanted to be late for class, her only choice was not to listen to the messages until she came home from work that night.

Shouldering her bag, she took one last look at

the blinking light on her machine and headed out the door.

As she hurried from Sparrow Hall along the path on the academic quad, Jenna relished the unusually warm day. She really didn't feel like going to class, or working for that matter. *How many days as nice as this are we gonna get before next spring?* she thought.

But guilt won out—she had to go to class.

As she entered Bransfield Hall, she passed two girls chattering excitedly. Jenna heard only a snatch of their conversation, but it was enough to grab her attention.

"Murder . . ." was the first word she actually heard.

Jenna blinked and focused on the girls. One of them was vaguely familiar but she couldn't place her. The other was a willowy redhead with a pleasant smile.

"You're kidding. On campus?"

"Last night," the other confirmed. "Some girl."

"God, what a semester," the redhead said. "First that professor goes psycho, and now this. My mother's going to pull me out of here if we have any more of this crazy sh—"

The door clicked shut behind them.

Jenna felt sick.

A murder on campus. She instantly focused on the two killings the previous week, and wondered if it had been the same killer. Perversely, she found herself almost hoping that it had been some kind of lovers' quarrel. That would be easier than the dread of knowing a serial killer was lurking around somewhere close.

In class, Jenna was greatly distracted. Eventually she started to drift. Thanks to the unseasonably warm weather, and the sun streaming in through the windows, Jenna felt her eyes flutter several times, her head bob once. Then she sat up straight, embarrassed.

Her mind wandered back to murder. She hoped she wouldn't have to assist in an autopsy this afternoon. She just didn't feel up to it. Normally she didn't work on Tuesdays, but Slick and Dyson were still backed up with reports.

Then another thought entered her mind. If someone had been killed on campus, Danny might be around. *Every cloud has a silver lining,* she thought, and then grimaced at her own callousness. Still, the thought of seeing Danny made her brighten up.

Older man or not, impossible object of affection or not, the thought of him made her smile.

When Jenna arrived at Dr. Slikowski's office, about twenty minutes past two, it was empty. It was a relatively common occurrence, but she was relieved. Either Dyson and Slick were off on other business, or they were down in the basement performing an autopsy.

Quickly, she checked to see if either of them had left her a note. No note meant she could immerse herself in transcription and computer records, return some of the office calls, answer the phones . . . all things she could do without utilizing much brain energy.

All things I can do without handling anybody's internal organs.

It was too beautiful a day for the dead.

There were no windows in the outer office, only in Slick's office. But enough sunlight splayed through the open door to satisfy Jenna. She even went in and cracked the window a bit to let in some fresh air.

For more than an hour she worked diligently. The phone rang only twice, and she stepped out of the office just once, to get a can of soda.

At a quarter to four, the phone rang again.

"Pathology," Jenna answered. "Dr. Slikowski's office."

"Hello, Jenna, it's Audrey Gaines," said the familiar voice on the phone. "Could I speak to the M.E., please?"

"Oh, hi, Detective," Jenna replied. "I'm sorry, but Dr. Slikowski's not in at the moment. Can I take a message?"

There was a moment of silence on the other end of the phone. Then Audrey gave a soft, almost inaudible sigh.

"Detective Mariano and I were hoping we could schedule a meeting with him, as soon as possible," Audrey explained. "In fact, we were sort of hoping to come by at about five o'clock. Is there any way you can track him down, and get back to me with a confirmation?"

"I can try," Jenna told her.

Since she hadn't heard from either Slick or Dyson, she had to assume that both were down in autopsy. She could have just called down but figured it wouldn't hurt to make an appearance before she left.

When she hung up the phone, Jenna picked up her Sprite and headed down the hall to the elevators. *Well*, she thought, *it's almost over.* She had told Dr. Slikowski she could work only until five o'clock, mainly because she had to get some work done on her Rasputin paper for Professor Georges. But now there was a slight chance she'd get to see Danny, which would be a bonus.

One of the fluorescent lights in the basement corridor was flickering, and Jenna blinked. It bothered her eyes. Then she was past it, and moving down the hall toward the autopsy room. She reached the door, and took a sip of her soda before pushing it open.

Dyson smiled as she entered. Slick was busy, his head down, and he barely noted her presence.

"Didn't know if we'd see you today," Dyson said. "Getting a lot done?"

"Yeah, without you to . . ."

Jenna's voice died.

The can slipped from her grasp and thunked to the floor, sticky soda spilling out in a pool by her feet.

Dyson had a set of lungs in his latex-gloved hands. Other organs were spread out on the scale. The corpse on the table had its chest opened down the middle, a gaping hole with broken ribs exposed. Dr. Slikowski was using a scalpel to make an incision just below the hairline, slicing the flesh on the face.

Melody's face.

Jenna screamed, one hand coming up to cover her mouth, as if that might stop the scream, stop it all from happening. Tears sprang to her eyes. Then both hands slid up and twined in her hair, and she closed her eyes, unwilling or unable to look.

She felt like she might throw up.

Then Jenna collapsed, slid down to the ground to sit, holding her head in her hands, whispering the word *no* over and over again. She didn't know how long she went on.

Sprite soaked through the seat of her cargoes. She never felt it.

Jenna was numb. Slick and Dyson were as kind as could be, but she was only peripherally aware of talking to them. Of them helping her. Of Dyson offering to call her father, or walk her back to her dorm. She didn't know what she'd said, how she convinced them that she'd be all right—particularly when she couldn't possibly believe it herself—but eventually, she left Somerset Medical Center.

The sun cast long afternoon shadows across the campus.

It was a beautiful day.

Tears streamed down Jenna's cheeks and she held her arms tightly around herself and shivered against a chill that was only on the inside. Nothing in her life had prepared her for this. Nothing had ever happened to her that was even remotely as hurtful, as horrible.

She could barely breathe.

Only when she reached the front door of Sparrow Hall and looked up at the windows of the third floor did she realize that her pain, her horror, was selfish. There were worse things than what she had experienced that day.

"Hunter," she whispered.

Her face crumbled, and she had to lean against the door for support as fresh tears coursed down her face. She cursed God and prayed to him at the very same time, but mostly, she just asked him, *Why?*

There was no answer.

Barely aware that she was moving, Jenna found herself upstairs on the third floor. She moved past her room. She crossed the common area and went on to the boys' side of the floor. At Hunter's door, she paused only a moment before knocking.

Jenna held her breath and tried to compose her face.

The wound was too fresh.

The tears would not stop.

Yoshiko opened the door, and it was obvious she had been crying as well. Hard tears, that made her eyes red and her cheeks puffy. Seeing her made Jenna cry all the harder.

Then Hunter was there, getting up from his bed, moving toward her.

Jenna choked out his name, but couldn't manage anything else. She opened her arms and Hunter moved into them. Together, they sobbed, and then Yoshiko joined them in their embrace, in their pain.

Finally Jenna said the only thing she knew to say. "I'm sorry."

The car weaved through the back streets of Somerset toward Interstate 93. Outside its glass and steel, the world kept turning; life went on with all its usual vibrant chaos. But inside the car, all was still and dead. The world had, for all intents and purposes, ended two days before with the discovery of Melody LaChance's body.

Jenna sat in the passenger seat as Pierce drove, his eyes on the road, hands too tight on the steering wheel. He had clicked the radio off the instant he'd started the car. No one had commented, but Jenna had silently agreed—this was no time for music. There was no place for music in the world now. Not today.

In the backseat, in the quiet that was being generated by the individual thoughts and shared grief of the car's passengers, Hunter sat with Yoshiko. Yoshiko looked at him from time to time, but Hunter never met her gaze. She held on to his hand, and though he never pulled it away, he never squeezed her fingers to let her know that he felt her pain and sympathy.

Pierce guided the car up the on-ramp and headed south toward Boston and Logan airport.

Hunter was flying home today, going back to Louisiana to attend his sister's wake and funeral. The knowledge that Melody was also flying that day—her body in a box in the hold of the plane—haunted him. It wasn't right that an eighteen-year-old should have to accompany his much-loved sister's corpse home.

But it wasn't right that she should have had her heart torn out, either.

It wasn't long before the sign for the Callahan Tunnel and the airport came up. Professor Logan had lent Pierce and Jenna his car for the trip. Hunter had tried to demur, but Yoshiko had told him that he really did not want to take a taxi. Jenna wouldn't have allowed it.

Still, it was as quiet in the car as it would have been if he had taken a cab. Quieter, perhaps. Jenna decided that was all right. Maybe it was just what Hunter needed. To share in silence what could never really be shared.

Certainly, they all had their own grief—Melody had been Jenna's best friend, after all. Now Jenna was all jagged glass and tears inside. And Yoshiko had been a friend to Melody as well. Then there was Pierce. He and Melody had just started . . . something. But all of that pain would have to wait. It was all put on hold until Hunter's plane left the ground. They were there to see him off, not knowing if he'd be back that semester . . . or at all. For the moment they had to swallow their own pain and be there for him.

Which was precisely what they did.

They left the car in short-term parking, and Pierce carried one of Hunter's bags to check-in. Only ticketed passengers were allowed past the security checkpoint. Jenna thought it was a cold and soulless place to have to say good-bye.

So there, among the rushing travelers, Hunter turned to face his friends, his dead sister's friends, and he nodded silently. His jaw was thrust out a bit, as he hardened his features, doing his best not to cry. Jenna realized it was the first time she'd ever thought he didn't look like a boy.

Hunter was a man now. Death had done that to him.

Pierce hung back as Jenna and Yoshiko hugged Hunter in turn. Yoshiko held on to him for a few seconds extra, and Jenna saw Hunter bite his lip a bit, saw his face tighten with the powerful emotions he was holding so close. Then the moment had passed.

"Our hearts are with you, Hunter," Yoshiko told him. "Please call."

"Is there anything we can do?" Jenna asked. "I mean, while you're gone?"

Hunter looked at her, then at the rest of them.

"Just don't ask me if I'm all right, okay?" he said almost sternly. "Don't ever ask me if I'm all right."

Hunter was about to pick up his carry-on bag when he noticed Pierce, still hanging back from the others. He stepped forward, the young man whose sister had been sickeningly murdered, and held out his hand.

"Thank you," he said to Pierce.

Pierce lifted his chin, stood a bit straighter, every inch the marine. He took Hunter's hand and shook it firmly.

"I'm very sorry," he said.

Hunter nodded. "I know."

Then he was gone, walking through security and toward his gate. Toward home, where his world had shrunk to two, his mother and himself.

Jenna hadn't even reached the electronic doors to the outside when she had to stop to wipe away her tears. Suddenly she could barely breathe. There was a pain, real pain, not something imaginary—a tightness in her chest. And yet, there was no physical reason for it.

A tender hand landed on her shoulder, and Jenna peered into Yoshiko's beautiful, delicate face, ravaged by grief. The two girls fell into each other's embrace, and just held on.

Pierce stood by, placed a strong hand on his sister's back, and waited in silence, not mouthing any empty assurances that it would all be "all right." Jenna was glad of that.

When she glanced at her half brother, she saw how cold his face had become. His features were almost cruel in their lack of expression. *But his eyes . . .* They were different. There was a spark there, a tiny glint of something dangerous.

Pierce Logan was angry, and it occurred right then to Jenna that he had the training to do something about it.

It had been only ten years since Danny Mariano had graduated from college. Not a very long time in the scheme of things. But every time he drove onto the campus of Somerset University—walked among its students—he was reminded of that decade. The odd thing was, he didn't really feel any older, and for half a second, he would feel at home, as if he were returning to a comfortable place, as if he were one of them. Then he would realize that they didn't see him ten years younger. They saw Danny Mariano as he was now.

It created a vast distance between them.

It made Danny Mariano feel old.

But he wasn't old. Thirty-one wasn't even middle-aged. Thirty-one was really very young. Most of the time, that speech worked. But sometimes it made him feel even older.

Now, for instance.

Danny rapped on the glass at the door to Sparrow Hall. Behind the security desk a male resident assistant looked up from a political science textbook. Though it always made him feel silly, Danny flashed his badge and I.D., and the kid's eyes lit up as he rose to open the door.

"Can I help you?" asked the R.A.

"You already did," Danny told him.

Before the kid could ask any other questions, Danny walked off down the hall. He thought he heard the kid start to say something, but he must have thought better of it, because the last sound he heard was the front door clicking shut.

Danny reached into the pocket of his canvas jacket and pulled out a scrap of paper. On it, he'd scrawled "Sparrow Hall, Rm. 311." He stuffed it back into the pocket, reminding himself that it was getting a little chilly for this coat, and he'd need to start wearing his leather, or get something else.

As he marched up the stairs, his mind wandered to Audrey, and the things she'd said about his interest in Jenna. Audrey was wrong, no question about that. Jenna was a kid. Cute and smart as hell, but still just eighteen years old. Still, he wasn't exactly doing anything to dispel Audrey's insinuations by coming here tonight.

He'd been by Dr. Slikowski's office again, trying to see if the M.E. had come up with anything the cops had missed. Audrey and Danny had been trying to come up with some kind of common denominator among the victims—family, friends, work, interests, education—but they hadn't had any luck at all. The profile from the FBI hadn't arrived yet.

Slick didn't have anything new for them, either.

Albert Dyson had told Danny that Jenna hadn't been at work since the day she'd walked in on her friend's autopsy. Danny couldn't blame her, but he'd been hoping to run into her. Still, the M.E.'s office was close to Jenna's dorm.

Which brought him here now.

He stepped through the door onto the third floor, and into chaos. Someone was blasting Barenaked Ladies down the hall, and Danny suddenly felt a little less like an old man. He owned a copy of the album that was playing. *Of course, I still think of it as an "album," so that doesn't help much.*

Profanity and the Morse code of college cool was scrawled on message boards on doors up and down the hall. He passed a pair of guys in ragged clothing, both walking with a kind of lazy stoop that made him smile to himself. They were doing their best to seem like slackers, but here they were at one of the best non–Ivy League colleges in the country.

In the common area, half a dozen students were loudly arguing Middle Eastern politics, smoking, and drinking beer. The school had a policy against alcohol, of course, not to mention that most of them were probably underage, but Danny wasn't about to arrest them for being college students. As he passed them, a British-accented kid with bleached-blond hair waxed poetic on the "demonization of Muslims."

The girls' end of the corridor was entirely different. The message boards were still laced with jargon and profanity, but there was a general orderliness about things that he appreciated. The world, he had often thought, would be a much better place if women were in charge of everything. He'd been told several times that his attitude was "nouveau sexist," but he hadn't quite known how to respond. Last time, he'd just said, "Thanks."

At Jenna's door, he raised his right hand and, after only a moment's hesitation, rapped with his knuckles.

"Just a sec!" came a shout from within.

A moment later the door swung open. Jenna wore a long blue T-shirt with the Superman *S* emblazoned across the front over a pair of pastel-striped pajama bottoms. In the eyeblink before she realized who was at her door, Danny registered the grave cast of her features, the pinch of her lips.

Then she blinked. Her eyes widened and she blushed a bit as she leaned toward the door, obviously wanting to hide behind it but too self-conscious to do so.

"Oh, God, Danny," she said quickly.

"Jenna, hi," he said. "I'm sorry. Obviously I'm catching you at a bad time."

She grinned, and he was happy to see that she was still capable of doing so. "What?" she asked innocently. "You don't think this is a glamorous ensemble?"

"I know, I know," he said, "you'd like to thank the Academy . . ."

Jenna executed a short bow. Then she rolled her eyes, and Danny realized how often she did that. It was very self-deprecating, and Danny thought it was probably a defense mechanism.

"Well, come in, already," she said, and stepped out of the way.

For the barest moment, he hesitated. Then Danny stepped over the threshold into Jenna's room. It was actually pretty orderly, for a college dorm room, but there were stacks of books on the floor, and jackets and other articles of clothing hanging about. There was a huge poster of Hawaii on one wall, which reminded Danny that Yoshiko was not there.

"Where's your roommate?"

"Out with friends," Jenna replied. "She'll be back by eleven, though."

There was an odd tone to her voice, and Danny frowned a bit at it.

"We're calling in these days," she said. "Checking in, I should say. Coming in when we say we'll be here. So we won't worry about each other, more than we have to."

Danny nodded. "That helps, I guess."

"What would really help is knowing the killer is gone. Or, even better, dead in a gutter somewhere."

Though he was a bit taken aback by the bitterness and anger in Jenna's voice, Danny understood it. Her best friend had been murdered horribly. And what she'd seen in that autopsy room . . . no one should have to see someone they love like that. Not ever.

"We're doing all we can," he told her.

Jenna fidgeted, raised her hands and dropped them helplessly to her thighs. "That wasn't a dig," she said.

"I know."

"So are you going to tell me what you're doing here? Or do you usually make a habit of visiting girls' dorm rooms late at night?" Jenna teased.

Danny sputtered a moment, unable to form a response to that.

Jenna laughed at him. "Not that there's anything wrong with it," she added. "I'm sure your nocturnal visits are usually very welcome. Like Batman."

With a chuckle, Danny shook his head. Jenna was trying for the amusing banter they'd shared in the past. But her heart was clearly not in it. So, rather than come up with a witty response, Danny just got down to it.

"Actually, I came by to—"

" 'Cause, y'know, I already talked to one of the other detectives," she said. "They were questioning all of Mel's friends, I guess trying to see if there was anything weird going on. But nobody knows anything. Nobody saw anything."

"Except Hunter," Danny reminded her.

"Right," Jenna agreed. "Our little red raincoat boy. So we know the killer could be a white guy, maybe six foot, with short, darkish hair. That narrows it down."

Danny sighed. Her anger and frustration and pain were burning so strongly that he dared not get too close.

"Maybe I should come back another time," he suggested gently.

Jenna faltered then. She moved back into the room, to the chair by her desk, where she sat in front of the glow from her computer screen, surrounded by her books and puzzles and assorted pictures of her mom and her friends from home. There were new photos there, of her with Yoshiko, and Hunter . . . and Melody. Sitting at her desk, surrounded by her stuff, was the most comfortable spot in the world to her.

"Sorry," she said. "I didn't mean to be—"

"Don't be," Danny told her. "I get it. Actually, the whole reason I came by was to say that I'm sorry. I know you two were close. I assumed it would be a while before you went back to work—if you go back to work—and I just wanted to give you my condolences."

"Thanks," she said, nodding. "It's great of you to come by."

"The least I can do." Danny just stared at Jenna for a moment, wanting to say or do something more to comfort her. She seemed so vulnerable, and he didn't miss the irony of the symbol on her T-shirt. He felt the urge to hold her, but that was strange territory, too close to Audrey's earlier commentary. *It's not my place. I'm already doing everything I can.*

"Well, there is one more thing you could do," Jenna said, eyes darting around the room now.

"What's that?"

"Ever since Melody . . . since last week, my brother's been like a zombie. He looks like he hasn't slept in days, and he's completely distracted. I'm worried that . . ."

"What?" Danny asked, curious.

"He's a marine, Danny. Pierce is in counterintelligence. He was falling for Melody pretty hard. I guess I'm afraid he might be, I don't know, out looking for the guy."

"You mean literally?" Danny asked. "Playing Guardian Angel on campus or something?"

Jenna nodded. "I haven't seen much of him, but if you run into him . . . I just don't want him to get hurt."

"Of course not. But your brother's a military officer, Jenna. He knows better than to get involved with something like this, no matter how deeply it has affected him. If you talk to him, please tell him he can come see me anytime. I'll give him all the information I can, but he's only going to get himself or someone else hurt if he goes cowboy on us."

"Cowboy?" Jenna asked, screwing up her face at the unfamiliar expression.

"Sorry," Danny said. "Vigilante. If Pierce starts to act like some kind of Old West gunslinger, he's going to get himself in trouble. You don't think he has any firearms, do you?"

Jenna shook her head. "I haven't seen him with any. I hate to say this, 'cause it'll sound like melodrama, but I don't think Pierce would need a weapon."

"Point taken," Danny said. "Thanks. I'll try to keep him out of trouble."

"Thanks," Jenna said with a genuine, soft smile that made Danny's mind drift for a moment.

Then he blinked. *That was dangerous.* They said their good-byes and Jenna offered him a weak half smile as she shut the door behind him. As he went down the stairs, his mind was awhirl with thoughts about the murders, and about Jenna. He reminded himself not to forget about her brother. As soon as he had the chance, he was going to try to have a talk with Pierce Logan.

The last thing they needed was a decorated Marine Corps officer playing cowboy with a serial killer.

On Wednesday night, nine days after Melody's murder, Jenna and Yoshiko sat in The Cuckoo's Nest, having the hottest buffalo chicken wings in all of creation. Pierce sat across the table from them, eating a burger and drinking Corona beer, a taste he'd picked up on the West Coast.

"So the show is just canceled?" Jenna asked Yoshiko, somewhat stunned.

Yoshiko shrugged. "What can they do? Hunter quit. They could get someone to fill in for Rolf, but the role of Maria was too big. They could recast and postpone, but apparently everyone agreed that it was better to scrap it after what happened."

That last bit hung in the air for a moment. Pierce took a long swig of his beer. He hadn't said much during dinner, but Jenna was glad she'd been able to get him to come along.

"Hunh," Jenna grunted. "So he's really coming back?"

"Sometime next week, I guess," Yoshiko replied, obviously as surprised as Jenna was. "I only talked to him the one time, but he said he didn't want to spend the rest of his life half a year behind. I told him we'd pick him up, so I guess we'll hear from him when he's ready."

"He should take his time," Jenna said. "I know he doesn't want to lose a semester, but he shouldn't come back until he's ready."

Yoshiko was nodding in agreement when Pierce spoke up.

"What about you, Jenna?" he asked.

She looked at her brother, and for the first time in a long time, she saw softness in his eyes.

"I'm all right, I guess," she said.

"You're sure? You guys were tight. All I'm saying is, if you're having a hard time, you know your professors would give you incompletes. If you're finding it difficult to focus."

Jenna blinked. Stared at him a moment. "You and Dad are talking again, I take it," she said.

"Some things are more important than personal politics," Pierce told her. "You're sure you're all right?"

Jenna glanced over at Yoshiko, who was also looking at her with concern. She was grateful. Of course so much focus had been placed on Hunter, and both of them had their own pain to deal with, that she'd received little consideration. It would have been selfish of her to expect it. But she was glad of it now.

"I'm okay," she said. "I think I've actually been keeping my mind off it by studying instead. Haven't missed a class. I'm even going back to work on Friday."

Yoshiko frowned. "Jenna, do you think you should—"

"Should," Jenna replied firmly. "Very should. If I don't, I may never go back. And it's something I want to do. Besides, it'll make me feel like I'm helping, somehow. Being a part of the team, or whatever."

"It's not like you haven't been doing your own research," Yoshiko said.

Jenna nodded unhappily. "Yeah. For all the good

it's done. I've been Net girl for a week. Thank God there are so many newspaper and TV news archives online."

"Have you found anything useful?" Pierce asked.

Jenna shook her head. "You'd be disgusted by how many murders involve some kind of mutilation. Let's just say a lot. A percentage of those involve the removal of organs. I haven't found anything exactly like the work our heart thief is doing, but I haven't given up yet."

"What I don't understand is . . . I mean, why would anyone take a heart?" Yoshiko asked with a little shudder of revulsion. "I can't say I connect with the mind of a serial killer, but . . . why take it with you?"

"Dr. Slikowski says there have been a ton of documented cases of serial killers saving bits of their victims. I guess the common wisdom is that they do it to have a trophy."

"That's so sick," Yoshiko whispered.

They were quiet again then. Jenna figured the others were thinking exactly what she was: that the killer had taken part of Melody as a souvenir of some sort.

"Why not something smaller?" Jenna asked suddenly.

They both looked at her. Pierce stared with particular intensity.

"What?" her brother asked.

"No, listen," Jenna said, though nobody had contradicted her. "He may wear a raincoat so he can wipe the blood off, or whatever. Maybe he puts his . . . oh, God—trophies—in a pocket. But a human heart is huge."

"Says the girl who holds them in her hands three days a week," Yoshiko added with a grimace.

"Why not something smaller?" Jenna repeated.

They all thought about it a moment.

Pierce tilted his head thoughtfully.

"What?" Jenna asked him.

"Maybe he's not keeping them," Pierce suggested slowly. "There have been cultures throughout history that adhere to various beliefs regarding the consumption of human flesh. There are or have been people who believe there are real health benefits in eating human organs. Never mind the huge body of spiritual thought regarding the gaining of another's strength—both spiritual and physical—through the consumption of their flesh."

Both girls stared at him in horror.

Yoshiko spoke up first. "You think this guy is *eating* the hearts of his victims?"

Pierce shrugged. "Just a thought."

"A hideous thought," Jenna chided.

"For all of us," Pierce acknowledged. "But if we want to stop this son of a bitch, we have to consider everything.

"*Nothing* is impossible."

chapter 8

On Friday afternoon, as she walked along the quad toward the Somerset Medical Center, Jenna felt a fluttering in her belly. The cold rain spattered off her umbrella, but she was oblivious to the weather. She had another concern—she was jittery, and she didn't want Dr. Slikowski or Dyson to see just how jittery she was.

Not that she didn't expect them to be sympathetic. She knew they would be. It was simply that she didn't want them to coddle her. She wanted to be treated as a colleague, rather than a student.

But the thought of stepping into an autopsy room, of holding human organs in her hands, of watching as a corpse was explored for clues to its demise . . . the very idea of it made Jenna's breath catch in her throat. It made her shudder with dread.

Still, she had to do it. She had only been at this thing a little over a month, but already she had come to feel that it was what she was meant to do. It wasn't medicine, not the way she'd always imagined it, but that was all right. It was, to her mind, a valiant occupation. There was also an element of police work, of investigation, that intrigued her. What had happened—Melody's murder—was horrible. Debilitating. But if she allowed it to turn her from the path that seemed to call out to her, that would be a tragedy as well.

She hurried across Carpenter Street, feet splashing in a puddle, soaking the leg of her jeans. Jenna ignored it. Her mind was elsewhere. There was something else, another reason she needed to get back to work. Her thoughts flashed back to the expression on Pierce's face the day they'd dropped Hunter off at the airport; his look of grim determination that said he was going to do something about this. They had not spoken of it, and Jenna had purposely avoided asking Pierce what he was up to.

The police were doing their best. Jenna was sure of that. But it was her half-formed opinion that police work sometimes led to circular thinking. Collected wisdom on a subject might lead detectives in one direction, without allowing them to investigate another.

Jenna wasn't going to leave it at that. She wanted to make sure the heart thief was caught and punished. Part of her hoped that he'd catch a bullet when they finally brought him down. Either way, Jenna wouldn't rest until she was certain he wasn't going to murder again.

It was with all of this in mind—anxiety and intensity—that she walked into Dr. Slikowski's office on the second floor of SMC. Dyson was on the phone in his cubicle, gazing intently at his computer screen. He dragged the fingers of his left hand through his curly black hair and leaned back in his chair.

As he did so, he noticed Jenna.

"Hey, Gina, can I get back to you?" he said into the phone. "Great. Later today, yes. Bye."

Dyson hung up in a hurry and stood, pushing back his chair as he moved toward her, eyes sympathetic.

"Hey, Jenna," he said gently. "I didn't expect you in today. How are you?"

"I'm doing all right," she lied. "At least, I've stopped seeing her when I dream."

He blinked, then offered a soft smile. "It's good to see you."

"You too," Jenna agreed. Then she let her guard down, allowed a long sigh to escape her lips, and sat down in his chair. "I just needed to come back, Dyson, y'know? If I don't start beating the horse that threw me, I don't know if I'll ever be able to do it."

"That's 'get back on' the horse that threw you," Dyson corrected.

"I don't ride horses," Jenna told him. "But I can dish out a mean whuppin' if I have to."

Dyson laughed at that, shaking his head, and—much to Jenna's relief—the cloud of awkwardness that had hung between them dissipated.

"There *is* a lot to do," Dyson admitted.

"Great," Jenna said. "Let me get started, then. Just as soon as we have coffee. Assuming you want coffee."

"I want an I.V. drip of espresso. But regular old petrol will do."

"You got it," Jenna said. "Let me just see if—"

Jenna abruptly stopped speaking when she saw Dr. Slikowski, sitting in his wheelchair just inside the door of his office. The M.E. gave his wheels a push, and glided out into the outer office.

"Dr. Slikowski," Jenna said by way of greeting. "Can I get you some coffee?"

"No, thank you, Jenna," he replied sternly. "Nor do I think you ought to be getting coffee for Dr. Dyson. I believe that when you suggested you return to work today, I told you that I would have to consider it."

Jenna frowned and stared at Slick's face. His wire-rimmed glasses were high on his nose, and his aquiline features and short, grayish hair gave him a vaguely birdlike appearance.

"Right," Jenna agreed. "So here I am. To talk to you, I mean. I'm fine, boss. Really. I'd like to get back to work."

Slick sighed. He reached up under his glasses and rubbed his exhausted eyes. When he looked at her again, it was with obvious sympathy, but also with a certain amount of disdain.

"Go home, Jenna," he told her. "Give it another couple of weeks, and then we'll try again."

Jenna's mouth fell slack, her lips parted slightly in astonishment. After a moment, she managed a "But." After which, half a minute went by in silence.

"I want to get back to work," she said at length. "I think maybe I *need* to get back to work."

Slick looked down, licked his lips as he seemed to be considering her words, and then he finally raised his head to regard her again.

"I'm sorry, Jenna," he said. "You're just too close to this. I want you to come back—Lord knows we need you. But I'm not sure how much good it would do any of us for you to come back now. When this heart thief business is over, I'll welcome you with open arms.

"But for now, I don't think it's healthy for you to be here."

Jenna stared at him for a long moment. Then her expression changed to one of anger and frustration. She took a quick glance at Dyson, who only gave her a slight shrug, but said nothing.

Without a word, she walked out.

On the short walk back to Sparrow Hall, she forced herself not to cry.

*   *   *

"Can you hack in?" Jenna asked hopefully.

Yoshiko pulled one leg up under her butt and chewed on her lip a bit as she stared at Jenna's computer screen. They had an unspoken agreement that they'd use Jenna's PC. If there were any repercussions, they shouldn't fall on Yoshiko. It was all Jenna's plan to begin with, though Jenna was sure that Yoshiko was with her one hundred percent. *She wants to get the son of a bitch just as much as I do,* Jenna thought.

A lock of hair fell across Yoshiko's eyes, and she blew it off her face. She wore silk pajamas that had been a gift from her mother on her eighteenth birthday, and Jenna had coveted them since the first time she'd seen Yoshiko wear them. But, then, Yoshiko always seemed to look good. *A Hefty bag would look good on her. Evil woman.*

"It isn't like television," Yoshiko told her.

"Could you possibly repeat that one more time?"

Yoshiko arched an eyebrow and shot her a daunting glance. "I'm trying to help, here."

"I know," Jenna said, sighing.

"It's set up so that the docs can access records from outside the system," Yoshiko confirmed. "Problem is, unless you have a password, or there's a simple back door in the system, *we* can't access it from out here. And *you* can't go into the office."

Jenna paced and thought. She stopped in front of the mirror and stared at the dark circles starting to form under her eyes. *Great,* she thought. *Wonder*

Woman I'm not. She'd been keeping up with classes, despite everything. Or mostly keeping up. But between that and trying to deal with all of this—sleep hadn't been easy to come by.

Suddenly Jenna blinked and smiled to herself. Yoshiko noticed.

"What is it?" she asked.

"Okay, Slick is a bit of a stiff, right? He's going to have some kind of pseudointellectual password, or something personal, or the name of some jazz musician I've never heard of. But he's going to go to lengths to keep it private, because that's the way it ought to be."

"And?"

"Well, Dyson isn't half as concerned or half as uptight as Slick. Plus, he's kind of spacey, right? So he's probably going to use something he already uses elsewhere. He told me once that his bank card and his home security alarm code were the same as the phone number his parents had when he was a kid. It was the only way he could remember it all."

"But we don't know that number."

"True, but it wouldn't be a number. At least, I don't think it would. It would be something he connects with work in his head. Something simple."

Yoshiko looked at the screen thoughtfully. "So, what, then? C-O-R-P-S-E?"

Jenna barely noticed the humor. She was thinking. Then she had it.

"His e-mail addy," she said. "I don't know what

he uses at home, probably the same thing, knowing him. But at work, it's *fuzzydys*."

Yoshiko blinked, a smirk on her face. "Fuzzy dice?"

"Dyson. He's got this really curly hair. Fuzzy. D-Y-S. Fuzzydys."

With a shrug, Yoshiko said, "We'll try it." She typed the letters, and hit the Enter key; a moment later the screen changed. "We're in!" Yoshiko said excitedly.

"Good," Jenna said, without pleasure.

Yoshiko turned to her curiously. Jenna was not excited. She was not smiling.

"Download everything there is on Melody's autopsy, and the other two heart thief victims, too," she said darkly.

"No problem," Yoshiko confirmed. "But what then, Jenna? I mean, isn't Slick, like, the wizard of dead things? What are you going to find that he hasn't?"

Jenna shrugged. "Maybe nothing. But he works with cold, hard facts. He's a scientist. I'm not. Maybe some of the research I've done on mutilation murders or whatever will pan out. There's got to be something that's linked to something else.

"I don't want anybody else to have to go through what happened to Melody."

On Saturday morning Frank Logan sat at his kitchen table eating breakfast with his son, Pierce.

There had been a great deal of sorrow in the house in the past week, and previous to that, a great deal of rancor. The two men were at odds politically.

But Frank knew that now was not the time for politics. Since Melody LaChance's murder, he'd kept his opinions to himself. They hadn't discussed it, but he knew Pierce appreciated the space. His son had been keeping very late hours, and he couldn't help but be distracted and concerned by Pierce's nocturnal wanderings.

They didn't talk about it. It wasn't their way. Instead, in the absence of arguments or heart-to-heart discussions, they were left with a third topic: Jenna.

"She's all right, Dad," Pierce said as he forked a bite of French toast into his mouth. When he'd swallowed, he continued, "She's a bright kid, and brave, too. She'd make a good marine."

Frank looked up at Pierce in horror, only to breathe a sigh of relief when he saw the mischievous smile on his son's face.

"Very funny."

"I thought so," Pierce agreed. "Seriously, though. She's a big girl."

Frank nodded. "I guess that's part of what's got me concerned. I had such high hopes for us when I found out she was coming to Somerset. And we have been able to spend some time together, mostly meals of course. But I thought it would be different."

"You thought she'd be here all the time, asking you for answers," Pierce observed.

"You're not far off," Frank confessed.

Pierce sipped his orange juice and regarded his father over the rim of the glass.

"You missed that part, Dad," Pierce said. "She doesn't see her mother hardly at all now. You're getting more than that—you should be glad. An eighteen-year-old college girl doesn't have time for parents. She's too busy learning how to have a life."

Frank smiled. "When did you become so *wise?*"

"The Corps'll do that to a man," Pierce said. "Semper Fi."

With a deep sigh, Frank said, "Let's not start that again, shall we?"

Before Pierce could reply, the doorbell chimed. Frank frowned, then rose from the table. Pierce waved him back to his chair.

Through the frosted glass of the door, Pierce could see two figures on the front porch. He unlocked the door and pulled it open, blinking back the sunlight.

"Good morning, Lieutenant Logan," said a reasonably attractive woman with a hard set to her jaw.

Then the two of them flashed their badges.

"Lieutenant, I'm Detective Mariano, this is Detective Gaines," said the other visitor. "We're investigating the death of Melody LaChance. If you don't mind, we'd like to ask you a few questions."

Pierce heard movement behind him and saw that his father had come out into the hall.

"Audrey, what's going on?" Frank asked.

The fact that his father knew these detectives was not lost on Pierce. Nor was the lack of response from Detective Gaines, or the guilty expression on Detective Mariano's face.

"I'm more than happy to cooperate," Pierce told them. "But I gave a statement last week."

"Audrey?" Frank prodded.

"We'd like you to come with us, Lieutenant Logan," Detective Gaines said, ignoring Frank. "It won't take long. Just a few questions."

"Then you can ask me here," Pierce said angrily.

"Damn right," Frank grunted.

Which was when Detective Mariano stepped forward, too close. Into Pierce's personal space. If he hadn't been a cop, Pierce would have physically removed him from that space. But it solidified in him an abiding dislike for the man. Given a chance, they'd come to blows. He'd make sure of it.

But not now.

"Don't make this difficult, or embarrassing," Mariano said. "If you cooperate, it will go much easier and faster, and we won't have to wonder what's holding you back."

Pierce glared at him.

"Stay put, Pierce," his father told him. "You don't have to go anywhere."

"No, I don't," he replied. "But if my going means

they'll stop wasting their time on idiotic tangents and get down to finding Melody's killer, I'll be more than happy to cooperate."

Instead of backing up, Pierce stepped even closer to Mariano, staring down into the shorter man's eyes. Their noses were perhaps three inches apart. To his credit, Mariano held his ground.

Pierce grunted. "I'll get my coat."

Orrin Balch had been homeless for more than two years. He had lived on the streets of Boston for most of that time. In the past few weeks, however, he'd begun to spend most of his time in Porter Square in Cambridge. It wasn't anywhere near as overrun with other street people as most of Boston was, which meant people were by turns either colder or kinder.

More important, he'd discovered a cubbyhole out of sight beneath the enormous escalator in the Porter Square T station. Twice, he'd gotten guff from the security guards, but once they saw how truly inconspicuous his little hidey-hole was, they left him to it. Kind of them, really. They could get in trouble for letting him bunk down there, and they did it anyway.

Truly kind.

With one of the singles he'd received while turning in his change at the bank, Orrin bought a token for the T and descended the long escalator. He prayed that his bedroll, which he'd daringly left in his Spot, would still be there. With relief and a great deal of pleasure, he found that it was. It would be so nice not to have to lug it with him on his rounds.

Orrin kept an eye out, waiting until a train came to take the commuters away from the platform and there weren't many new folks coming down the escalator. The guards were nice enough to turn a blind eye to his secret Spot. He was going to give them the courtesy of not being too obvious about it, so as not to get them in trouble. Plus, he didn't want anyone coming along and claiming his Spot.

As soon as the coast was clear, Orrin ducked under the escalator. Sighing, he settled down with his packages, which included a load of takeout from the Dragon Light Chinese restaurant a little ways out of Porter Square on Mass Avenue. An order hadn't been picked up, and the kitchen help had been more than happy to give it over to him rather than throw it away.

All in all, it was turning out to be one hell of a week.

Orrin slid backward on his bedroll, making room to spread out the food. But when he put his hands behind him for support, his left hand landed on something hard and rubbery and greasy. Wincing with disgust, he wiped that hand on his pants and turned to peer into the folds of the bedroll to see just what it was.

For the first time since he'd been a child, Orrin Balch screamed.

It was a human heart. Gray in spots, as though it might be rotten or diseased. But that wasn't the worst. The worst was the way it had been torn at, as if animals had gotten to it.

That was it, he suddenly understood. Animals. Some dog or other must have gotten down here, left this little prize in his bedroll. All he had to do was dump it in a trash can, and then . . .

Which was when he heard the security guards trotting beside the escalator. His scream had brought them running.

"Damn," Orrin muttered angrily. "Now I'm gonna lose my Spot."

chapter 9

chapter 9

Danny Mariano hated Monday mornings. Not for the same reason as everyone else in the world, however. Cops didn't work the traditional Monday through Friday, nine to five, so there wasn't any of the normal Monday resentment. As far as Danny was concerned, each day was either a day he had to work or a day he had off.

But he still hated Mondays, because though to him it was just another day, to the rest of the world it was an excuse to bitch about heading back to work or school after having blown a weekend and not gotten anything done. The world was cranky on Mondays, and Danny wasn't a big fan of cranky. Particularly because it sort of infected him. Which made him even crankier. A vicious circle.

Still, all in all, and despite the fact that the Somerset P.D. was in the middle of an investigation involving a serial killer—an investigation that had forced them to work with the Cambridge P.D. and would probably have FBI mooks bragging about their expertise inside of a week—despite all of that, Danny was pretty up.

The gallon-size jug of Colombian blend from Starbucks would do that to just about anyone.

It was almost eight-thirty when Danny walked up the stairs to the squad room. He hadn't seen Audrey's car in the lot. It was only the second time he had ever beaten her into "the house"—and both in a single week. Audrey had always prided herself on being the workaholic among them, so Danny looked forward to busting her chops. As he entered the squad room, he unzipped his brown leather jacket and was about to set his cup down to take it off when he glanced across the room.

Jenna Blake was sitting in the worn chair next to his desk.

Immediately, Danny's adrenaline started pumping. Forgetting his jacket, he moved quickly toward her.

"Jenna, are you okay? What happened?"

She glared at him, and Danny froze in place, ten feet away from her. Jenna pushed herself up out of the chair as though she might tear out his throat. Danny blinked and took a step back.

"What happened?" Jenna cried. "What happened? That's a good goddamn question, Detective!"

Danny bent his head down. He knew what this was about. When he looked back up, Jenna was biting her lip, staring at him with red eyes, blinking, nostrils flaring with rage.

"Jenna, you have to understand—"

"What?" she snapped. "That you're a bastard? That you're the kind of guy who'll go to someone—someone who's hurting and maybe needs a friend—and under some pretense of friendship, you'll try to make a case out of thin air?"

Danny narrowed his eyes. "That isn't true."

"Do you know how I found out you had dragged my brother down here for questioning?" Jenna said, her voice practically a whisper. "My brother and my father didn't want me to know. They wanted to keep it from me. I had to find out from my mother, who let it slip by mistake. Do you have any idea how embarrassing it was, to know they were trying to keep it a secret from me? Trying to protect poor little me?"

The squad's lieutenant entered the room, followed closely by Audrey. Danny glanced over and Audrey shot him a look he couldn't read. But it wasn't good, that was for sure.

"Look, Jenna, let's talk about this in the break room, all right?" he said, not really giving her a chance to answer.

Danny grabbed her elbow and started hustling her toward the door, but Jenna shook him off.

"Yeah, right," she muttered. "I don't want to embarrass *you*, God forbid."

Once he'd gotten her into the break room, little more than a large storage closet with a table, two chairs, and a couple of vending machines, Danny shut the door and turned on her quickly, before she could get going again.

"Why don't you tell me what you're so pissed off about," he suggested sternly.

She looked as though she might attack him. "You *used* me," she said. "Got me talking about Pierce without bothering to tell me that he might be a suspect. I mean, I know we don't know each other all that well, but I thought we were friends. That I could trust you. I just thought that we . . . I don't know *what* I thought."

"You *can* trust me," Danny told her. He hadn't failed to hear the uncertainty of her words, her desire to express something about their mutual attraction, and he was glad she'd refrained. He didn't think he could handle it right now, and it wouldn't be fair of him to brush it off.

Now she only watched him, not bothering to tell him how ridiculous she obviously thought it was for him to claim that she could trust him. At length she brushed her auburn hair away from her face and glanced around the room.

"Is my brother a suspect?" she asked, as if it meant nothing.

When it meant everything.

"Of course he is," Danny said plainly. "I'd have to be stupid not to consider him a suspect."

Jenna's jaw dropped. She was about to protest when Danny held up one hand to stop her.

"Just listen," he said. "If I didn't trust you, and you couldn't trust me, I wouldn't tell you any of this. But listen. Please."

When Jenna didn't respond, he took that as a cue to continue.

"The murders began when Pierce arrived in town. He had no alibi for any of the three murders. He was dating one of the victims. He's a powerfully built guy, with military training. Plus, I questioned your friend Yoshiko as well, and the line of questioning led to her recalling that Pierce had discussed with both of you various reasons why someone might want to take human hearts."

"Do you realize how stupid that sounds?" Jenna shouted. "Come on, Danny, Hunter *saw* a guy in a raincoat going toward the auditorium the night that Melody was killed."

Danny shook his head and blew out a long breath.

"First, we don't know that the guy in the raincoat was our killer, and even if he was, there's no way to be certain it wasn't Pierce, since Hunter didn't see his face. Second, Hunter went back to his dorm before joining his friends that night, so he's a suspect as well."

Jenna stared at Danny in horror.

"I didn't know he went back to the dorm," she said.

"Yeah. His roommate told us that. I went easy on Hunter before he left for Louisiana. But I'll have to grill him hard when he gets back. Not because I want to, Jenna, but because it's my job. Do you get that at all? Do you think I wanted to bring Pierce down here? Right now, we don't have much, and he fits the bill. Doesn't mean I think he did it, but I can't ignore the possibility. Do you understand?"

Danny searched her eyes, eyes that stared at him as though he were some kind of alien life-form. Jenna shook her head slowly, and then tears sprang to her eyes. All the anger had left her, and she sat down in one of the ugly orange plastic chairs at the small table.

"Your job sucks," Jenna told him.

"Sometimes it does, yeah," Danny agreed.

"I feel sick."

"I don't blame you."

Danny moved toward Jenna, placed a hand on her shoulder, hoping to soothe her, to comfort her in some way. She looked up at him with her red eyes and tears, so beautiful and vulnerable and yet so brave and determined. For a moment he could not breathe.

Which was when Audrey pushed open the door to the break room with something that barely resembled a knock.

"Danny, we've got a . . ." Audrey's words trailed off midsentence.

Suddenly very aware of his hand on Jenna's shoulder, Danny managed to control his reaction as he pulled away from her and turned to face Audrey. He knew she was wondering exactly what she had just walked in on. For the first time, Danny didn't care. *Let her wonder*, he thought, tired of trying to explain himself.

It wasn't even nine in the morning, and he was exhausted.

"What's happening, Audrey?" he asked, not bothering to explain Jenna's presence beyond the argument Audrey had already seen when she first came into the squad room.

"We have a DOA in Lafford Square."

Danny nodded and looked over at Jenna. "We're catching this morning, Jenna. We can talk more later, if you want."

Jenna scowled. "I think we're done talking," she said, getting up from the table and brushing by him.

For a moment Danny was stunned. He'd thought they'd finished their argument, that she had begun to understand what he was dealing with. That he was only doing his job.

"Jenna—"

"I can find my own way out," she said, as Audrey stood aside to let her go. From the doorway she spoke angrily to him. "I told you I thought Pierce was trying to figure out who did this to Melody."

Danny couldn't respond to that. Not then. Instead, he just nodded. "Yeah. You did. Maybe you're right. Maybe not."

"Go to hell," Jenna said through gritted teeth.

Then she was gone.

Danny took a long breath, and let it out slowly, and threw his hands up in frustration. As he passed Audrey at the door, she opened her mouth to speak.

"Not a word," he told her. "Not a single word."

On his way down the steps, Danny zipped up his jacket. He hadn't even had a chance to take it off.

The DOA was in a parking lot behind the Somerset Theatre, an old-time movie palace that mostly showed retrospectives and film festivals. Currently they had a three-day Chow Yun-Fat festival going on. Danny thought Chow was just about the coolest guy on the planet, but now wasn't the time for displaying his love of Hong Kong action films.

There was work to be done.

He steered the car through the bizarre street layout of Lafford Square and into the lot behind the theater. There were two prowl cars already on the scene, lights flashing, and a third from the forensics unit. The officers on the scene had run yellow police tape around a Dumpster at the back of the lot, and a forty-something Asian woman was sitting on the curb not far away, her hands fluttering in the air as she spoke to one of the cops.

"The hell with Wheaties," Danny said, his voice

gruff with sarcasm. "This is the only way to start a day."

Audrey hadn't said much in the car, and she kept silent now. Danny wasn't going to let that bother him. There was nothing going on between him and Jenna Blake. She was only eighteen years old, and nothing was going to change that.

He kept telling himself that, and he knew that it was true. But a small part of him kept coming back to the anger in her eyes. He couldn't deny that it mattered to him that she was so furious, it mattered what she thought about him.

Audrey set off toward the uniforms at the crime scene, and Danny followed.

"What've we got, Teddy?" Audrey asked.

Teddy Collins, the officer she'd addressed, glanced around quickly, as if to see who might be listening before he responded. That was how Danny knew. It was that moment of hesitation that told him just what Teddy's answer was going to be.

"Woman on the curb, Mrs. Xin? She found the DOA. It's another one, Audrey."

Danny cursed under his breath, then ducked under the yellow tape and went up on tiptoe to peek into the Dumpster. The corpse was half covered by cardboard boxes, but part of his torso was visible. Broken bones jutted from the empty chest cavity.

"Phenomenal," Danny muttered. "I love Mondays."

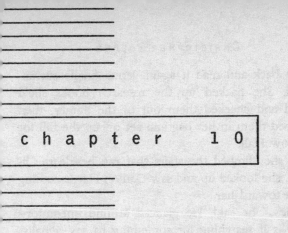

chapter 10

Monday afternoon, about the time Jenna would normally have been heading over to Somerset Medical Center for work, she wandered into the library instead. She still had a bit of research to do for her Rasputin paper.

Once inside the library, she tried to focus on her work, but without much luck. Her life seemed like one long nightmare lately, and it was getting to her. She stared at the words on the page before her, but couldn't make sense of them.

It's like I've been going around with my brain wrapped in a fantasy, and now it's been torn away.

For the first time she really understood that she didn't define the world around her, it was harshly defined all by itself, without her input or approval.

Barely able to read a single page without having

to go back and read it again, Jenna finally surrendered. She packed up the research books she'd found and checked them out of the library, then dumped them in her bag and set off up the hill for Sparrow Hall.

As she climbed the stairs that ran beside the library, she looked up and saw Damon Harris coming down toward her.

"Hey," he said. He glanced around uncomfortably, as if searching for something to say. Finally, Damon's gaze caught hers. "How you holding up?"

Jenna watched him closely, surprised and pleased by his concern and his directness. Most people just danced around Melody's death, or mumbled some kind of comment about it. Damon gave her the space to tell him how she was really doing.

But Jenna wasn't ready to do that.

"I'm all right," she lied. "Trying to bury myself in school." That latter part was at least half true.

Damon nodded. It seemed as if he were going to move on to another topic, but then he paused and tilted his head to one side. "How's Hunter?"

The two had never been close, but they lived on the same floor, all of them, and Damon knew Jenna and Hunter were friends.

"I haven't really heard from him," she said. "I've been too weirded out to call. But apparently he's planning to come back this semester. Maybe sooner rather than later."

"Damn, I don't know if I could do that," Damon

said, shaking his head. "Guy's gotta have serious guts to come back here. Give him my best if you talk to him."

"I'll do that."

Then Damon walked on, down the stairs toward the library, and Jenna started up the steps toward the chapel again. After a moment, she turned to watch him walk away, wondering why things hadn't worked out between them. *At least we're still friends,* she thought.

She wondered if Damon's friends had anything to do with the fact that things hadn't worked out. They'd had real problems with the fact that she was white. Not that it mattered in the long run. Neither of them had made any effort to continue dating. She couldn't lay it all on Damon. As for the future, though . . . *who knows?*

As she crossed the quad toward Sparrow, Jenna found her thoughts drifting again. From Damon Harris to Danny Mariano. You couldn't find two more different men. Particularly since one of them was actually a man, rather than an eighteen-year-old kid from Nowhere, New Jersey. She realized that, in spite of his looks and his smarts and his charm, there was still something about Damon that reminded her of guys from high school.

Danny, on the other hand . . . *is impossible,* her mind finished.

With that frustrating and confusing thought, she pushed through the door of Sparrow Hall and went up the north-side steps to the third floor. When she reached her room, she was disappointed to find that Yoshiko hadn't come back yet. Jenna had hoped they could have dinner together. It was just after five, though, so she resolved to wait a little while before heading off on her own. She dumped her bag and jacket on the chair by her desk, grabbed the book she'd been reading—Ellroy's *The Black Dahlia*—and flopped down on her bed.

Before her head hit the pillow, she saw the flashing light on the answering machine that indicated she had messages. Sighing, she sat up, walked across the room, and hit Play.

"You have three messages," the machine told her.

Message one was from her mother.

"Hi, honey. Mom again. Just thinking about you . . . worrying, as usual. Let's plan a day off together, soon if possible, okay? Some girl time? Oh, and don't forget next Sunday is your Uncle Brian's party. It would mean a lot to him if you were there."

There was a pause before her mother said, "I love you. Call me."

Jenna was torn. She loved Uncle Bri, and he *was* turning fifty, but she wasn't in love with the idea of going home just for that, and then coming right back to school. If she had a car she might not have minded so much. She resolved to ask her father if she could borrow his.

Beep! "Hi, guys, it's me."

Jenna sucked in a quick, short breath at the sound of Hunter's voice.

"I'm sorry I haven't called. I'm just trying to spend as much time as I can with my mother. I'll be back soon, maybe as early as Friday, but I'll call about the flight. I'd . . . if you want to call back, you can. It's okay, I mean."

He rattled off the number of his mother's house in Louisiana and Jenna jotted it down quickly. Instantly, she dropped the pen and reached for the phone.

Beep!

Jenna paused. She'd forgotten there was a third message.

"Hello, Jenna? It's Danny Mariano."

Jenna stared at the machine.

"I'm just calling to say that I'm sorry if you feel caught up in this whole thing, if it's making life difficult for you. But I also thought you'd like to have at least a little bit of good news."

He paused there, sort of chuckled derisively, and then sighed. "Maybe that's not the way to put it," Danny's message went on. "We found another victim today. I'll trust you to keep that to yourself for now, but what it means to you is that your friend Hunter is off our suspect list. Anyway, just thought you'd like to know. Take care."

Beep! "End of messages."

For a moment, Jenna smiled, relief sweeping over her. She reached for the phone again to call Hunter, though she wouldn't be so thoughtless as to share this news with him. Then, again, she stopped. A shiver went through her, and as it passed it took her smile and her relief away with it.

"Damn it!" she snapped, and glared down at the answering machine. "Damn you!" she swore, slapping the closet door beside the phone.

Hunter was off the hook. That was great news. But Danny didn't say anything about Pierce, which meant that he was still a suspect. And with Hunter cleared, that made Pierce an even more likely suspect.

Jenna was filled with a sudden, unreasoning fury at Danny. She let a stream of cussing fly from her lips. Then she ran out of steam and just leaned against the closet, sad and angry and afraid of what might come next.

Which was how Yoshiko found her a few minutes later. Jenna explained the whole thing to her, and it was Yoshiko who placed the call to Hunter. Jenna talked to him for a few minutes, lending him the support and concern that she knew he needed. But her mind was elsewhere, even then. On Danny, whom she had the overwhelming desire to scream at. But more important, on the heart thief; the sick son of a bitch who'd murdered her best friend.

Questions spun in her mind, most of them questions she'd asked herself in the past. But this time, they seemed more concrete. More legitimate. A fourth corpse had been found. Even now, it was likely being cut apart by Slick and Dyson. Organs being weighed. All but one.

There'd be no heart.

But why?

If the killer wanted a trophy, he could have taken anything. Certainly there were a great many small pieces of the human body easier to conceal and keep than a heart. She'd been doing the research into mutilation murders, and there was no question that Pierce's suggestion that the killer might be eating the hearts had lodged in her head. Maybe he was. But if so, then why? Pure insanity wouldn't necessarily account for it. What was the logic behind it?

Jenna was determined to find out.

As Yoshiko finished the call with Hunter and then pushed her out the door to Keates Hall for something to eat, Jenna's mind was awhirl.

She knew what she had to do.

It was after eight o'clock when Jenna used her key on the door to the medical examiner's office. She pushed in quietly and closed the door behind her. Slick's inner office door was closed, probably locked, but that didn't matter. She wouldn't need to get in there.

Quietly, glancing at the door to the hall several times, Jenna went to the cubicle where she had worked until this case had begun, and where she hoped to keep working when it was over. She realized, of course, that breaking and entering might jeopardize her employment, but it wouldn't be the first stupid thing she'd done.

Thanks to Yoshiko's hacking skills, she'd been able to access the records on the other autopsies from her dorm. But the lab results and the M.E.'s official reports hadn't been input yet, and the new one wouldn't have been transcribed this soon and certainly wouldn't be in the computer. Jenna knew that. It wasn't until she saw the stack of manila files on her desk, however, that she realized how true it was. It looked as if they were at least four days behind on their data entry, maybe more. No wonder Yoshiko's Net magic hadn't really paid off.

"Ha, you needed me," Jenna said, grinning happily as she sat down at the desk and started to flip through the folder on top of the stack.

"We certainly did."

Jenna spun, wide-eyed, knocking several folders off her desk and scattering papers on the carpet. Engaged as she was, she hadn't heard the click of the door opening behind her, or the soft hush of the wheels of Dr. Slikowski's chair on the rug. But there he was, just the same.

Slick leaned back in the chair, watching her, a small smile playing at the corners of his mouth. The dull fluorescent lights glinting off his wire-rimmed glasses made him look even more like one of his "patients" than usual.

"Can I help you with something, Jenna?" he asked, the irony thick in his voice.

"No, I . . ." She let the words trail off. Jenna couldn't meet his eye. "I'm sorry, Dr. Slikowski," she said, though she thought the apology sounded hollow. "It's just that—"

"That the police have not caught the killer of your dearest friend, and your brother is a suspect. That you're haunted by both these things, and you're not going to be able to have a single restful night until you've figured out what's going on, stopped the murderer, and cleared your brother. And that the taking of the victims' hearts strikes you as more than sadism and trophy keeping."

Jenna blinked. Sat up straight in her chair and stared across at him, this thin, bespectacled, graying, fortyish man in a wheelchair. Though he was kind, he'd always seemed so distant. But now, here, when the rest of the world outside the office door had gone home or gone on to other things, here he was speaking to her as though he could read her mind and her troubled heart.

Slick looked at her warmly. He shook his head and rubbed the circles under his eyes, then moved his chair farther into the room, turning so that he faced her more directly.

"Yes," she said. "That about sums it up."

"I'm sorry I've kept you away," he confessed and smiled again. "I really think you're better off not working in here, not doing what we do, until it's over. But I won't keep you out of the loop anymore.

"That was wrong of me."

"No, no, I understand," Jenna protested. "It's just that—"

"Let's not start that again, shall we?" Slick interrupted.

Jenna looked at him and blinked in surprise. "You're not angry that I'm here?"

Dr. Slikowski leaned back a bit in his wheelchair. He removed his wire-rimmed glasses, cleaned them with the front of his shirt, and slid them back on.

"I've given this a lot of thought, actually," he told her. "You're a very bright girl, Jenna. You've already proven that you've got a knack for getting at the truth of something. One day, if you decide to do so, you might make a decent medical examiner, but you obviously tend more toward the investigatory end of things.

"I should have known you'd continue to look into your friend's murder, and more than that, I ought to have welcomed it. It's personal for you, of course, and there's a great myth about why people shouldn't be allowed to pursue a dangerous course driven by personal interests. All of which is probably crap. You want to solve these murders even more than I do. Certainly, I can hardly sleep knowing someone else might be killed by this monster, but what I'm feeling . . . well, I can't even imagine how much worse it must be for you."

Slick took a deep breath and let it out, then he looked at Jenna expectantly.

"I . . . don't think I understand," Jenna said, bewildered.

"You want to help," Slick told her bluntly. "I should have let you. And it's not too late to start now. Why don't you pick up those files, and you can read about the John Doe they found today. Tomorrow afternoon, we'll talk a bit more about the case, and see if anything occurs to you that I haven't considered yet."

Jenna smiled with surprise and delight. "Thank you, Dr. Slikowski. Thanks for letting me—"

Slick waved her words away. "I admire your fortitude, Jenna. And it simply makes sense for us to share information, rather than work at cross-purposes."

He turned his chair, then, and headed for the door. "I'll leave you to it, and leave you to lock up if you don't mind. Obviously you've brought your key."

Jenna flushed with guilt, but Slick didn't notice. At the door, he was slipping on his headphones, and Jenna braced herself for the eruption of jazz percussion she knew would be pumping from his Walkman any second. But he paused as he put the headphones on.

"Nearly forgot," the M.E. said. "There's one thing I should tell you, that hasn't even made it into that pile yet."

"What's that?"

"A couple of days ago, the Cambridge police found a heart in the Porter Square T station. Discarded there. It belonged to the John Doe the Somerset police found this morning in Lafford Square."

Jenna frowned. "Discarded? Why would he throw it away?"

"Parts of it were quite diseased."

Even as his words sunk in and Jenna's mind began to go to the place she really didn't want to visit, to a truth she didn't think she wanted confirmed, Slick saved her the trouble. He said the words.

"He'd taken several bites out of it."

Jenna's stomach churned.

"He's eating them," she said quietly, as if the words would make it real, make it possible.

Pierce was right.

Tuesday morning Danny Mariano came into the office to find Audrey paging through a thick sheaf of papers.

"What've we got?" he asked as he pulled his jacket off.

Audrey read another sentence, then glanced up as his question filtered down through her concentration.

"Everything you wanted to know about our heart thief, at least according to the FBI profiling unit," she told him.

Danny nodded, for once grateful for the FBI's help. "Good. Anything we can use?"

"Just getting started. Pull up a chair."

So he did. They'd sent out all the details of the case to the profiling unit, the FBI's sort of all-purpose service center for psych evaluations of murderers who hadn't been caught yet. Danny had never trusted the idea that you could learn anything pertinent about a killer from a bunch of people making up stories about his past and present in a room somewhere in another state. But there was no question about it, the FBI profiling unit had a track record any detective would have to envy. They knew what they were talking about, and it would be foolish not to at least take their recommendations into consideration, particularly since they provided the profiling as a service to other law enforcement agencies. They did it as a favor, because it was their job to catch bad guys, just like it was Danny's.

So he spent an hour sitting across from Audrey and reading the pages of the profile over and over until it all became little more than a bunch of gibberish to him. They figured the killer was a white male, thirty to forty years old, with a competitive nature and a history of theft and physical violence. They suggested following up an investigative track on gambling addicts in the area, and noted that substance abuse was also likely in the case.

After an hour Danny put the pages of the profile down on Audrey's desk and pushed back to his own.

"I need coffee."

"I'll have a cup, since you're getting up," Audrey said idly, not even looking at him.

When Danny came back with the java, Audrey put the file down, stood up, and stretched. He handed it to her.

"What do you think?"

Audrey shrugged. "Some decent leads, things I hadn't thought of. But it just doesn't feel right to me. There's something we're really missing here. I think we need to start going back over possible connections among the victims."

"C'mon, Aud," he said, "we've been down that road a thousand times. There's nothing. Unless this John Doe turns out to have known all the others, then we've got something. Otherwise, *nada*."

"There is one thing," she said.

"What?" Danny asked, puzzled.

"They all had something he wanted."

Danny rolled his eyes. "Great. All four victims had hearts. Which narrows our list of potential victims down to every single person on earth."

Tuesday morning, Jenna didn't go to class. Since just after five A.M. she'd been sitting on the floor of her room with the autopsy records of the heart thief's victims spread out in front of her.

She was convinced there was something there.

It was just a matter of finding it.

* * *

Jenna and Yoshiko walked off campus to meet Pierce for an early lunch of pizza at Espresso's. Jenna hadn't seen him since before he'd been questioned by the police, and she felt oddly nervous about seeing him now. She reflected, as they walked along Carpenter Street toward University Boulevard, that she'd had so many pleasant ideas of what their time together might be like on this visit. Now, those hopes seemed ridiculous.

When they walked into Espresso's, Pierce was already there, sipping a Coke at the table where he'd first met Melody. Jenna didn't know if he'd realized it—assumed he probably had—and chose not to mention it.

He stood up as they walked over. Pierce's gaze flicked momentarily to Yoshiko, and he nodded his greetings with a mumbled "hey," and then looked back at Jenna. There were dark circles under his eyes from an obvious lack of sleep, but aside from that, Jenna was relieved to see hm. He looked as tough as ever. He'd even had his crew cut buzzed again, tighter on his head than it had been when he'd first arrived.

"Hey, little sister," Pierce said sadly.

"Hey, big brother," she said in return.

After an awkward moment they embraced. Pierce held her tightly, as though she were the only thing keeping him from falling down. Jenna hugged back. She was so worried for him.

"How're you guys holding up?" he asked as he

stepped back from her. He looked from Jenna to Yoshiko and back.

"We're all right," Yoshiko answered. "We talked to Hunter yesterday. He thinks he's coming back on Friday."

Pierce shook his head and let out a breath. "It's going to be so strange. I don't think I'll know what to say to him."

"Just say you're sorry," Jenna suggested.

For a moment Pierce's eyes flashed angrily, and then he shook his head once more. "Right," he said. "Of course. It's just, I feel like there should be more than that."

"It's all any of us can do for him right now," Yoshiko said.

"Hey, though, more importantly, how are *you* doing?" Jenna asked her brother.

"Me?" he said, without expression. "I'm in hell."

Jenna flinched and was about to reply, but Pierce just went on.

"This goddamn cop hauls me down for questioning, like I could have done this," he spat, growing angrier by the moment.

Jenna could see a vein in his temple start to throb. Yoshiko sensed his anger, and even backed up a step.

"Pierce," Jenna said and put a comforting hand on his biceps.

"With my record, my commendations," Pierce grunted. "How dare they? I mean, I was falling for her, hard. They could at least have paid me a little bit more respect, tried to follow up, tried to find someone who could confirm where I'd been. Now with this new one, that Gaines woman is all over me."

"Do you have an alibi this time?" Jenna asked gently.

Pierce glared at her. "What the hell's that supposed to mean?" he demanded.

"Nothing, I just . . . I was hoping someone could clear you of suspicion."

Pierce shook his head. "No. Worst part is, I was out and about at that time. Have been most nights lately." Suddenly Pierce lowered his voice and looked directly at his sister. "I'm trying to track the bastard down."

Jenna smiled. "Me, too," she said hopefully. "Any luck?"

"Nothing," Pierce said. "And I won't have anything if I can't get this cop to realize I'm not the killer."

Jenna winced. Looked away. She'd been angry at Danny, sure, but Pierce was taking things a bit far, in her opinion.

"He's doing his job, Pierce. Trying to find Melody's killer, just like we are."

Pierce froze. His eyes widened, then narrowed to a cold, furious stare.

"They always look at the boyfriend or whatever first anyway," Yoshiko said, not noticing Pierce's rage. "You showed up right when the killings started, and so far, no alibi. I'm sure they don't think you did anything, but they have to keep you on the list until they can . . ."

Yoshiko's words trailed off as Pierce turned his furious gaze on her. Then he looked back at Jenna. His nostrils flared as he spoke through gritted teeth.

"You can both go straight to hell," he snarled.

Then he stormed out of Espresso's, leaving both girls to stare after him.

"Wow," Yoshiko said quietly. "No wonder he's a suspect."

Jenna didn't have a response for that.

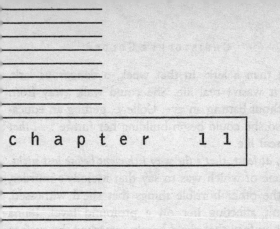

chapter 11

On Tuesday afternoon, as Jenna walked over to Somerset Medical Center, a very strange feeling began to settle over her. It took her a while to recognize that feeling as responsibility. Though the majority of her fellow students wouldn't have taken her part-time job if someone held a gun to their heads, Jenna hadn't thought of her work as a pathology assistant as all that different from other internships. For someone with her interests, it didn't seem any more unusual to her than a student who hoped one day to be a journalist interning at the *Boston Globe*.

In the past twenty-four hours, that had changed. Even the first week of school, when her life had gotten so insanely wrapped up in one of Dr. Slikowski's cases, Jenna had thought of the job as little more than a lark. In that week, a dangerous lark. Still, it wasn't real life. She could walk away from it without batting an eye. College, getting an education so she could begin building her future . . . *that* was real life.

Or, at least, that's the way I thought before last night.

None of which was to say that Melody's murder, and the other horrible things that she'd witnessed, weren't affecting her on a profound level. Jenna knew, in fact, that she'd barely scratched the surface of her grief. Before, she'd been someone to whom things happened, a bystander. Her conversation with Dr. Slikowski had changed her.

She had purpose now. She was part of it. Not a "kid" sitting in her dorm room tinkering with theories, but a member of the medical examiner's staff. Technically, she was part of the official investigation.

Jenna took that very seriously.

So it was with a grim set to her jaw and a great deal on her mind that she walked into the office after her class that Tuesday afternoon. She knocked before entering, out of courtesy more than anything, and then pushed the door open. Dyson wasn't at his desk, but the door to Slick's office was open and a kind of improvisational, hard-edged jazz poured out the door.

"Dr. Slikowski?" Jenna called as she walked toward the inner door.

Jenna poked her head in to see Slick behind his

desk. He was tapping on the desktop with a pair of number two pencils, and Jenna thought he looked almost maniacal. The man was normally quite reserved, and to see him drumming away like that was both charming and a little silly.

"Sorry," he said, dropping the pencils. "Sometimes it's the only way I can think."

The phone rang in the outer office.

"It's okay," he said, punching the Stop button on the small CD player in his office. "Let voice mail pick it up. Dr. Dyson is out this afternoon, and I already have one autopsy to perform today. If there's another coming, I don't want to know about it."

Jenna nodded. She knew that Slick liked to have Dyson there for autopsies. Though he'd never discuss it, there were a great number of things that were difficult for him to do from the chair, and Dyson had explained to Jenna early on that Slick didn't like to work with anyone he had to explain his needs to.

"I could assist at the autopsy, if you'd like," Jenna offered.

After a moment, Slick nodded. "You could at that," he said. "It'll be slow going, but I think we could manage together. And it would be easier than bringing someone new in to assist."

The phone stopped ringing.

"It's a domestic violence case," he explained. "Battered wife gave her husband what was coming to him with an aluminum bat, and then set the house on fire. I've got to determine what killed him, the bat or the fire."

Jenna winced at the mention of fire, instantly regretting her offer. The idea of being that close to someone who'd been burned to death repulsed her.

"I know you have to go through the motions," she said, "but really, what difference does it make? She killed him, right? One way or the other, she still did it."

Dr. Slikowski pushed the wheelchair back from his desk.

"True," he agreed. "But if he died in the fire, her attorney might be able to plead the charge down to manslaughter. If the beating killed him, that'd be different."

"Because the fire isn't a direct assault?"

"Exactly," Slick agreed.

Jenna took off her jacket. She glanced over her shoulder at her desk, where she'd sat reading files the night before.

"Any luck?" she asked, her gaze returning to Dr. Slikowski.

The M.E. lifted his chin, eyes narrowed in a questioning glance. Then he nodded.

"Oh, right," he muttered. "You know, Jenna, I'm sorry, but I've been so wrapped up in the cases that have come in over the past few days that I haven't really thought about it. I suppose I was putting it off in anticipation of your arrival."

Jenna shrugged. "Okay. I'm here."

"Yes, well, why don't we talk about it down-stairs?" Slick suggested.

A short while later Dr. Slikowski was closely examining the skull of the deceased wife batterer. The man's charred remains were awful to behold, and the stench was worse than anything Jenna had ever smelled, even with a mask on.

With Slick's careful instruction, Jenna was weighing and bagging the man's various organs, which had withered and dried out from the fire.

"So what do you think?" Jenna asked, disrupting the M.E.'s concentration.

Slick frowned. "Hmm?" he mumbled, glancing back at her. "Oh, we need to run some more tests, but given the lack of damage to the skull, and the condition of the internal organs, I think we'll find that he suffocated."

"What?" Jenna asked, incredulous.

"Well, the burns were severe, and the fire would have killed him eventually, no doubt," Slick explained. "But he was unconscious inside the house. There was no oxygen left in the room at all. His lungs were seared by flame, filled with smoke . . . he couldn't breathe."

"So manslaughter, then?" Jenna asked.

"Well, that's up to the jury, but my testimony will indicate that the smoke is what killed him. Which means that, though she obviously murdered him, it was an indirect sort of homicide. Given the severity of the domestic abuse, I'd be surprised if she spent more than a few years in prison."

Jenna nodded her head, blinking. "Wow," she said. "The entire case hinges on what you put in your report."

"Sometimes," Slick agreed.

"But you know," Jenna added, "that's not what I was talking about. When I asked what you thought? I meant about the heart thief."

"Bone saw," Dr. Slikowski said, slipping on the goggles that he wore for this part of the autopsy.

Jenna retrieved the instrument and handed it to him, careful to keep the black cable to the right of his wheelchair. The M.E. pressed a button, and the tiny buzz saw whirred into life. He brought the saw, whining like a dentist's drill, down onto the surface of the dead man's skull and began to cut straight across. After a moment, he paused and raised his goggles.

"As I said, I'm sorry I haven't put much thought into it today. However, I think what will help us more than searching wildly for answers is examining the questions."

"What do you mean?" Jenna asked, frowning.

Dr. Slikowski sat back in his chair.

"I've spoken to the Somerset detectives. Gaines and Mariano. You know them. Audrey tells me they're trying to use the FBI profile to get a fix on the killer's personality and motivations. Also, they're trying to find some kind of connection among the victims. They haven't had much luck either way. So something must be missing."

Jenna sighed. "Couldn't we just not have enough to go on yet?"

"Possibly." Slick nodded. "But with so many killings in such a short period of time, something tells me that we're missing an important piece of the puzzle. We need to know how and why he picks his victims. Barring an obvious clue to his identity, that's going to be how we figure out who's doing the killing."

"Well, we sort of know why," Jenna pointed out. "I mean, he's killing them to eat their hearts."

"But why these individuals?" Dr. Slikowski added.

"What would you normally look for in a pattern?" Jenna asked.

"Any number of things," Dr. Slikowski said, autopsy forgotten for the moment. "Lack of family or social connection among the victims seems to indicate a serial killer rather than homicide for gain. So we have to consider environment. Hunting grounds, if you will. In this case, they're quite varied. We also have to consider sex. And we do have two young, attractive female victims."

Jenna glanced away. *Mel* . . .

"I'm sorry," Slick said quickly.

"No, I'm okay. Go on."

"Well, we also have two middle-aged men," he explained. "So there's no sexually related pattern.

Nothing the police see. Nothing I see. Just this whole business with eating the hearts. So it would seem as if he's choosing people at random, killing them, and eating their hearts. Which hardly seems like something one would do at random."

Jenna nodded thoughtfully, remembering the report she'd read the night before.

"I agree," she said. "If it was that random, would he have thrown away that diseased heart?"

"Well, anyone would have seen that it wasn't a healthy heart," Dr. Slikowski explained.

"I know, but . . ." Jenna looked at him, frowned. "Can I just say 'yuck' that we're even having this conversation? But anyway, my brother was talking about primitive tribes who believed they would gain the strength of their enemies if they ate their hearts. Maybe there's something to that? I mean, the twisted psycho's not going to eat a weak heart, right?

"The guy obviously thinks human hearts are part of a balanced diet," Jenna went on. "But I've done plenty of Net surfing, and I haven't found much in the way of documentation on any belief in that. Not today. Okay, I mean, the ancient Mayans . . ."

Jenna let her words trail off. Dr. Slikowski was staring at her.

"Jenna?" he asked. "What is it?"

"Nutrition," she replied.

"I'm sorry?"

"He's eating them, right? And you just said the

big question is, Why them? Maybe it *is* them. Maybe there's something about these people in particular, something in their hearts or whatever, that he knows about, that makes them targets," she suggested.

Dr. Slikowski nodded slowly.

"It's possible," he confirmed. "Some kind of medical condition, or genetic predisposition, or something even simpler, that leads the killer to believe that their hearts are the most desirable."

Jenna watched as Dr. Slikowski put his goggles back on.

"How would he know that?" she asked, beginning to think her idea was nuts, though Slick obviously didn't think so.

"There are a million ways to find something like that out," the M.E. insisted. "It's probably nothing, but it isn't any crazier than a dozen other theories they'll be following up. The man is eating hearts, Jenna. That's psychotic enough, don't you think? Presuming there is a reason why he chooses specific hearts is not as far fetched as you'd believe.

"I'll finish up here," he told her. "I'd appreciate it if you'd go upstairs and pull the files on the four victims again, then put in a request for their personal medical files so we can see if there's any condition they share."

"Do you want me to call Detective Mariano?" she asked.

Slick shook his head. "Let's see what we find. I

didn't say it wasn't a crazy idea, only that it might be true. Let's figure it out first, shall we?"

Jenna smiled. The feeling she'd had when she first came to work that afternoon returned. She was part of a team, with a purpose. There was the possibility, even the expectation, that she could contribute something, accomplish something. She might be able to help bring down the man who murdered Melody.

Her smile disappeared, replaced by determination. It wasn't a game, she knew that. It had already cost her so very much. No, not a game. But it was a puzzle.

And puzzles needed to be solved.

To the renewed sound of the bone saw, she pushed out of the autopsy room and shut the door tightly behind her.

It was twenty minutes past five when Jenna stepped off the elevator on the second floor and started down the hall toward the medical examiner's office. There were no patients on this floor, it was all administrative, but it was busy just the same. Doctors, nurses, patients, salesmen, and secretaries filled the hall, coming and going. Most of them were going. Though a hospital didn't run on traditional hours, the office personnel tended to keep to the hours of a more familiar workday.

Jenna turned down the side corridor that led to Dr. Slikowski's office. Several people said good night as they passed, and Jenna returned the pleasant greeting. But her mind was elsewhere.

A woman with a mission, she thought. And knew it was true.

At the office, she fished out her key and let herself in. The lights were still on, and she went over to her desk, where she'd left her jacket, and slid into her chair. The files were laid out on the desk.

Open.

Jenna sucked in a quick breath, eyes darting around the office. She stood up quickly from the chair and it rolled back a few feet on the carpet. She put her back to the desk, to her computer, and glanced around the room.

I didn't leave the files open like that. But . . . the door was locked.

The only thing she could think of was that Dyson must have come back and been looking at the files. *How else would the door still be locked?*

Out of the corner of her eye, she saw something move. Jenna turned quickly to see her brother, Pierce, standing in the wide doorway to Dr. Slikowski's office. He wore a dark leather jacket and had his hands in the pockets as he leaned against the door frame.

"Hey," he said, as though his being there was the most normal thing in the world.

"Pierce? What the hell are you doing here?"

Even before the words were out, Jenna's mind

started to churn. The files were open. The door was locked.

"I told you I'm trying to find Melody's killer. I didn't think you'd copy the files if I asked you. Especially after our conversation at lunch today."

Jenna blinked. Backed up a step. "So wait, *I'm* the bad guy?"

"No," Pierce said coldly. "But neither am I. I couldn't convince you of that before, and I don't expect to be able to convince you of it now. If you're not going to help me, then I'm not going to ask for your help."

"You'll just take what you need?" Jenna snapped, growing angry now, stepping toward him.

Pierce practically growled at her. "I didn't come here for this," he fumed. "I was upset about our lunch and figured we ought to talk about it. I thought I'd come by and maybe we'd have dinner, and I could explain what I've been up to. Maybe you'd let me see those files."

Jenna nodded. It all came together pretty clearly in her mind.

"But nobody was around," she said. "So you used the training our hard-earned tax dollars have given you to break in and have a look around on your own."

"You've got it all figured out," Pierce told her.

"Damn right I do," she muttered.

But as she studied his face, the anger there, and thought again about the files and the locked door, she had to wonder. It was easy to believe him. It all made sense. Melody's death had hit him hard, and ever since, Pierce had been keeping very odd hours. It was easy, and much saner, to believe that he'd been out hunting for the killer himself, that he wanted to see those files to find out if there was anything he was missing.

That was the logical thing to believe.

But what if . . . ?

Those were the words haunting Jenna's mind. *What if it's all a lie?*

"I . . . Pierce, I think you should go," she said, blinking, stepping away from him again.

His anger visibly drained away. Twice, he opened his mouth as if he were going to argue, and then, finally, he threw up his hands, shook his head, and headed for the door.

"I can't believe you did this," she said as he passed.

"I don't have anything to say to that," he replied. "I'm just trying to do what I think is right. What has to be done. In time, you'll realize that."

Jenna shook her head. "Even if you're telling the truth—"

"If?" he demanded, staring at her. "As opposed to what?"

Jenna didn't respond. The hurt in his eyes was real enough that she didn't really think he was the killer.

But what if?

His behavior certainly wasn't helping her believe him. The benefit of the doubt only extended so far.

"Fine. You're trying to find the killer," she said. "That doesn't give you the right to do this. You could have waited for me, could have talked it out with me. Hell, you could be working with the police, for that matter."

"I'm sure they're just waiting for my help," Pierce said, as he pulled the door open. "You're so naive. Cops only want a case solved if they solve it themselves. They don't want the credit going anywhere else."

"That's ridiculous."

"Of course it is," Pierce said, shaking his head. "Doesn't mean it isn't true."

With that, he was gone, pulling the door closed behind him.

Jenna stared at the door for a long time. When she finally looked away, it was with a horrible roiling in the pit of her stomach.

Please, Pierce, don't do this to me. Please be telling the truth.

Jenna considered not telling Dr. Slikowski about Pierce's visit. She didn't want to tell him. And if it had just been something between her and Pierce, something *family*, she never would have said a word. Two things, two things in direct opposition to each other, made her speak up.

First, she didn't really believe Pierce was or could be the heart thief.

Second, she didn't really believe Pierce was or could be the heart thief.

Jenna didn't think her brother was a killer. But he was her brother, and that meant that somebody else would see things a lot more clearly than she would. Dr. Slikowski was not only the medical examiner, he was an expert on the science of death and murder, and therefore had plenty of experience in the matter.

So when he came up to the office after completing the autopsy they'd begun together, Jenna told him about Pierce's visit.

She never expected him to call the police.

At least, not right away. Not before we'd at least talked about it, tried to figure out what might really be going on.

But he didn't wait.

"They're probably going to arrest him, now," Jenna said angrily, almost sulking, as the M.E. hung up the phone.

"As well they should," Slick said angrily.

When she shot him a withering glance, his own stern expression softened and he took a long breath.

"Jenna," he said. "I'm not suggesting your brother's a killer. And I'm certainly not going to prosecute him for breaking in here, though if he weren't your brother, of course . . . But if he's truly got nothing to hide, a short conversation with the police shouldn't bother him. At the very least, they ought to know he's poking around in this case."

"*I'm* poking around in this case," Jenna said tartly.

"*You* work for *me*, and it's my *job* to poke around in this case," Slick replied abruptly. "Now, did you have an opportunity to request those files?"

Jenna shrugged. "You won't need them."

"I'm sorry?" Slick frowned. "What have I missed? In order to test your theory about the killer's eating of the victims' hearts—"

"It's blood type," Jenna told him. "They all have the same blood type. I ordered the files anyway, just to see if there's more. But they share the same blood type."

"I'll be damned," Slick muttered.

They sat in silence for a few seconds. Finally Jenna sighed, stood up, and grabbed her jacket.

"I need to go home," she said. "This is all getting too weird for me."

"I understand," Slick replied, as though she'd given him a choice. "But you have to know you did the right thing. You'll see. It's best the police know what he's been up to. If Pierce is attempting to find the killer, he could be putting himself in terrible danger."

Jenna chuckled at that. Though they'd never discussed it in detail, it was pretty clear from some of the conversations she'd had with Pierce that working counterintelligence meant the marines had trained him in both self-defense and some *serious* offense. They'd trained him to kill.

Compared to a marine CI officer, some serial killer in a raincoat is an amateur. But that didn't mean she wasn't afraid for him.

No matter how she looked at the situation, whether Pierce was telling the truth or not, Jenna felt as if it was all spinning out of control. She couldn't help but feel that the dying wasn't over yet.

And there's nothing I can do to stop it.

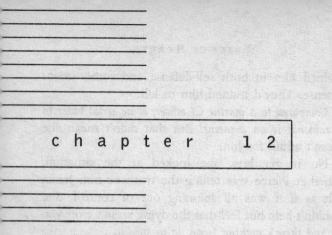

chapter 12

He hadn't been invited to the party, but that was all right. It wasn't really an "invitation" kind of thing. In the Greek system—the national fraternities and sororities—it was pretty much open house. Like tonight.

The girls of Alpha Omicron Pi had posted flyers all over campus. Not only was it a sorority party of enormous magnitude, not only did it celebrate the birthday of AOPi president Kiera O'Neil, but it was a charitable fund-raiser for Somerset Medical Center's Breast Cancer Awareness program as well.

Drunkenness for a good cause. At first, he had been quietly appalled by the whole thing. But then, as he sat and sipped a beer on the front porch of the AOPi house, which was on the corner of Alfe and Carpenter, three blocks from the hospital, he'd begun to mellow. These kids weren't doing anybody any harm, and it *was* for a good cause.

Several of the sorority sisters had eyed him suspiciously. He was obviously older than everyone else there, and he didn't go inside, just sat on the porch. A couple of times, partygoers had gathered near where he sat, and he'd been drawn into their conversations. But not for long.

He was waiting. Searching every face that passed. Looking for the right one. And, under the heavy sweater he wore, and the dark-brown canvas jacket, the bayonet's metal scabbard felt cold against his skin.

But not as cold as he was inside. He didn't think that was possible.

He heard whispers off to his left, and then a girl's voice, and a single word. "Him?" More whispers, angry this time, and he looked up to see two sorority girls studying him. When they looked away he studied them. Both had black hair, but were so different otherwise. One had olive skin, almost exotic, and the other was fair and delicate. Beautiful girls, but he felt nothing.

They weren't what he wanted.

As he watched, the girls' attention was drawn suddenly out to the road. He followed their gaze, and saw a blue sedan crawling slowly down the street in front of the sorority house. Prowling.

When the siren chirped and the red lights began to swirl in the rear windshield of the car, he didn't react at all. He'd known the moment he saw the car that it was the police. And it was simple enough to put two and two together.

He glanced angrily at the two girls on the porch, but already they were moving anxiously back inside the house. Several other partygoers followed. The rest of the students on the porch put their beers down quickly, surreptitiously—logically coming to the conclusion that the police had come to break up the party. They drifted down off the porch and started up Carpenter Street, back toward campus proper, their eyes not even straying toward the two plainclothes officers who stepped out of the car and headed up the walk toward the sorority house.

He found the entire scene fairly amusing.

The cops stepped up onto the porch. By then, he was the only person left outside. He took a long swig of his Corona and leaned back in the chair, regarding the pair of faces now examining him.

"Enjoying the party, Pierce?"

His eyes narrowed. Pierce swallowed and stared at the detective who'd spoken.

"You have a way of bringing any party to a screeching halt, Mariano. Gotta be your scintillating personality."

Mariano's partner, Detective Gaines, glanced from Pierce to Danny. "Knows you pretty well, doesn't he?"

Pierce had almost decided that he liked the woman. Then she pushed back the edge of her jacket to reveal her holstered weapon. It was done with practiced nonchalance, as if she didn't even realize she was doing it. But they both knew it was a reminder of just who was in charge.

The one with the gun.

In Pierce's experience, that was almost always the case.

Almost.

"So are you going to break up the party?" Pierce asked, offering a polite smile. "These kids aren't really hurting anyone."

"No," Danny agreed. "They're not. What about you, Pierce? Are you hurting anyone?"

Pierce's smile disappeared. He knew that his expression had changed, that he looked angry, but he couldn't help it.

"Not yet," he replied.

"Wrong answer," Gaines told him. "Please stand up, Lieutenant Logan. You're under arrest."

As the woman began to read him his Miranda rights, Pierce's eyes widened. "Arrest for what?"

"Stand up," Danny Mariano insisted.

But he was a good cop, and a smart one. He didn't grab Pierce. Instead, he too pulled his coat open to reveal his holstered weapon. But this was very deliberate. He unsnapped the safety strap on the holster, and stared at Pierce.

"I have the right to know why you're arresting me," Pierce said, without standing.

"Breaking and entering," Danny replied.

For a moment Pierce could barely breathe. Jenna had reported him. He'd explained to her what was going on, and she had told the police that he'd broken into Dr. Slikowski's office.

"I'll be damned," he whispered to himself.

"Perhaps," Detective Gaines said. "Now stand up and turn around; place your hands behind your head."

She drew her weapon.

Pierce sighed, stood up slowly, hands out in front of him. "I should probably tell you that I'm carrying something you'd probably consider a weapon."

The cops exchanged a glance he had trouble reading, and then Mariano spun Pierce around. He pulled Pierce's hands behind him and cuffed his wrists. Then the detective patted him down, and immediately found the sheathed blade snapped onto his belt at the small of his back.

"Jesus," Gaines muttered. "Okay, let me get this straight. You don't consider this a weapon?"

"It's a collector's item, actually," he explained. "M84/98 bayonet. The Germans used it for about thirty years, up until World War II."

"And you collect these?" Gaines asked skeptically.

"It's a new interest of mine," Pierce told her.

Both detectives glared at him. Then Mariano grabbed him by the shoulder and by the chain between his cuffed hands, and began to propel him down the steps of AOPi house and toward the car.

"We're going to have a little talk," Mariano said grimly.

"Yeah," Pierce told him, his voice cold. "And when we're done, I'm gonna have a talk with my little sister."

"Where the hell are we going?" Audrey Gaines stared at her partner, waiting for an answer.

Danny kept his eyes on the road. He'd been quiet the entire time they'd been in the car after picking Pierce Logan up. They'd spent almost an hour cruising the Somerset campus earlier, looking for the guy, only to have the complaint called in from that sorority party. *Convenient*, Danny had thought. But now . . .

"Shouldn't we be questioning our suspect?" Audrey prodded.

"About what?" Danny asked, shrugging. "You know as well as I do that Slick isn't going to press charges, and with Jenna being the only witness . . . she isn't going to testify against her brother. The DA isn't going to do a damn thing with a B and E case on a marine counterintelligence officer, when nobody wants to press charges and nobody's willing to put him on the spot."

Audrey sighed. "Danny. Hello? The B and E was a convenient excuse, but that's not why we arrested him."

"Of course not," he replied. "But we've already

questioned him about the murders, and I don't think we're going to get anything more out of him."

"So why is he still in lockup? Why don't we kick him loose?"

Danny shrugged again. "Let him sweat a while. We'll question him again, and we'll get nothing. We might be able to get him on a weapons charge, if he didn't buy that bayonet today, but if he did . . . point is, we've got nothing and he knows it. We'll question him, then we'll kick him loose."

Audrey was silent a moment as Danny turned from Cataldo Avenue onto University Boulevard.

"But first?" Audrey asked.

Danny nodded. "But first I want to talk to Jenna."

Audrey didn't reply. Danny glanced over at her, and saw the concern and disapproval on her face.

"Logan thinks she narced on him," Danny explained. "You heard what he said. I just think somebody should tell her that before he's back on the street."

"There's that," Audrey admitted. "But there's also the fact that you don't want her mad at you for arresting her brother?"

Danny braked, pulled the car to a stop at a red light. He looked over at Audrey, growing angry.

"We've been through this, Audrey," he said. "Girl's eighteen. All right, I like her. But it isn't like that; not the way you think you've got it worked out in your head."

Audrey nodded slowly. "Maybe. And maybe you

weren't paying attention the day I taught you not to get too close to a case."

He didn't have anything to say after that. They rode in silence until Danny pulled up behind Sparrow Hall and stepped out of the car. He left it running and slammed the door. Audrey didn't move.

"So, what?" Jenna asked, staring incredulously at Danny Mariano. "You think I'm in danger? From my brother?"

Danny looked at the floor, guilt covering his face. Jenna just kept staring. She couldn't believe it. When he'd come to the door, she couldn't have been more surprised, or embarrassed. She was in a cotton nightshirt with teddy bears on it and ragged sweatpants. Not exactly haute couture. But she'd been waiting for Yoshiko to come home and watch the movie they'd rented. It was a mountain-climbing movie, of all things. *K-2*. But it had Michael Biehn in it, and Yoshiko had a thing for "her Michael." The movie wasn't really the point.

Yoshiko was due home anytime now, but Jenna sort of wished Yoshiko was around, so she wasn't alone with Danny. Not that she was afraid of him or anything. It just always felt strange, being alone with him.

Strange enough to make her blush.

But the red in her cheeks now wasn't blushing. It was anger.

"Well?" she demanded.

"Look," Danny said slowly, "I didn't come up here to make you mad."

"No, you came up here to tell me you're going to release my brother, and you think I should be worried that he's going to come hunt me down because I *told* on him? Do you know how that sounds?"

Obviously exasperated, Danny threw up his hands and walked toward the door. He started to reach for the knob, but paused and turned toward her again.

"Let me ask you something," he said.

Jenna glared.

"Are you absolutely certain he isn't the guy?"

She opened her mouth to respond, to snap angrily at him, but then she hesitated. Faltered. Jenna closed her mouth, and dropped her gaze, eyes glancing about the room.

"He's my brother," she said at last. "I can't believe that he'd . . ."

She let her words trail off.

"I didn't think it was him before tonight," Danny told her. "Now I think it could be. I just want to make sure you're taking it seriously."

"Oh, I'm taking it very seriously," Jenna told him, not meeting his eyes. "I can't . . . I won't believe that Pierce killed Melody. But my best friend is dead, Detective Mariano. How could I not be taking that seriously?"

The expression in Danny's eyes was soft and comforting, but when he spoke, it wasn't to soothe her pain.

"Just be careful," he said.

Then he pulled open the door, slipped out, and closed the door tightly behind him as he left.

Alone in her room, Jenna went over and lay down on her bed. She wanted to slide under the covers, but in some strange way, that would have seemed like hiding to her, like surrender. Softly, she began to cry into her pillow.

Oh, Mel, I wish you were here, she thought, heart aching. *You'd help me figure out what to do.*

Jenna had never missed anyone so painfully. Never lost anyone so horribly. Every time she thought she had it beaten, every time she thought she had her emotions under control, the pain came back even worse.

God, it hurts.

But crying made it a little better.

A short time later Yoshiko came home, apologetic and bearing snack-type groceries. She saw Jenna's red eyes, and they hugged and talked for a little while. Then they put the movie on and, together, admired Michael Biehn.

Jenna did her best not to think about what was lurking beneath the tears, haunting her every waking moment now. That horrible question, made even worse by Danny's visit.

What if?

*   *   *

On Wednesday morning, Jenna was late for her biology class. Professor Lebo scowled at her, but said nothing, for which Jenna was ridiculously grateful.

I don't think I can handle getting yelled at today.

Particularly not after her conversation with her mother that morning. Not that April hadn't been sympathetic. Jenna's mother could get pretty wrapped up in work, but she was always cool, rational. Life had been going by a mile a minute, and Jenna hadn't had much time to miss her mother, but at times like this, she realized how much she did—miss her. All of her private thoughts, Jenna had always shared with her closest girlfriends, Priya and Moira. But when it came time to get serious, and make decisions, her mother was always there for her.

She always understood. But that didn't mean she agreed.

Like this morning.

"Jenna, you know how sorry I am about Melody," her mother had said. "I told you that you could come home for a while, and I still want you to consider it. But I also think you should try to take a step back and look at what's going on in your head.

"I'm not telling you to forget about what the police say," April told her. "But listen to your heart. Pierce isn't my son, but he is your brother. That means he gets the benefit of the doubt. But, unfortunately, it doesn't mean he's above suspicion. You can't know what's in any heart but your own."

"I'm just so confused," Jenna had told her, guilt already weighing her down.

"Call him," her mother had said. "No matter what, he deserves that at least. I'm not saying that telling Dr. Slikowski about Pierce's breaking in was the wrong thing to do. You did what you had to, and Pierce was definitely in the wrong there. But he's your brother—talk to him."

All through biology, and through most of Spanish, Jenna turned that over in her head. The last thing she wanted to do was talk to Pierce at the moment. But her mother was right. Between the pain of Melody's murder and the gruesome circus that everything else had become, she'd sort of lost touch with reality. Not that she was going to discount the possibility that Pierce could have done all this. But he was her brother, and she owed him the benefit of the doubt until she had reason to believe differently.

So when Spanish class ended, instead of stopping at Morrissey Hall for lunch, Jenna trudged past the building and over to her father's apartment. She rang the bell three times before her dad answered. He had a mug of coffee in his hands, and she had the idea that she'd interrupted his lunch.

"Jenna, what's wrong?" he asked the instant he saw her.

"Nothing's wrong, Dad," she said, and didn't

even sound convincing to herself. "I just . . . I wanted to talk to Pierce. Is he around?"

"No," her father said. "Hasn't been around much, in fact."

Frank looked away, eyes blinking several times, and Jenna thought he looked as though he'd done something wrong and didn't want to admit it. Then she began to wonder if it were she who'd done something wrong, or if there were another topic he'd rather not discuss.

"Did he come back last night?" she asked.

"Why don't you come in," her father replied, and stood back to let Jenna pass him. He closed the door, and they stood together in the foyer, staring at each other awkwardly.

"Dad—" Jenna began.

"No," Frank said, stopping her. "You don't have to say anything, Jenna. Pierce is my son. You're my daughter. He shouldn't have broken into Walter's office. He shouldn't have been carrying a knife last night—"

"What?" Jenna gasped, eyes wide.

Frank looked at the floor. "Ah. I guess you didn't hear about that, huh?"

"Dad, what's going on here?" she asked, more confused than ever.

"Pierce says he's trying to find the killer," her father explained. "I have to believe him. It's just that, well, the way he's going about it . . . if he'd just talk to someone, cooperate a little, he could shake this suspicion, get the police looking for the real animal behind all this."

"Then why doesn't he?" Jenna asked, almost angry at Pierce for being so stubborn.

"He wants to find the guy himself. Doesn't want the cops involved. Which makes me wonder if he doesn't intend to kill the man when he finds him," Frank said, shifting uncomfortably.

Jenna let that sink in for a few seconds. Then she shook her head, chewing her lip. "I just . . . I don't know what to think. But, I guess . . . I mean, you believe him, right?"

She searched her father's eyes for an answer.

He didn't turn away. Frank Logan looked his daughter right in the eye and didn't flinch.

"I have to believe him," Frank told her. "He's my son."

All through her international relations class that afternoon, Jenna couldn't get her father's words out of her head. Not just his words, either. *The expression on his face. I can't stop thinking about that look.*

Somewhere in the midst of the professor's lecture on Nixon's trip to China, Jenna realized that, for her, it wasn't just about finding Melody's killer anymore. It wasn't just about solving the puzzle and preventing future murders from taking place. Now it was also about proving that Pierce wasn't the killer. Proving it to the police. And to her father.

And to myself.

That was still the subject foremost on Jenna's mind when she entered Somerset Medical Center that afternoon and took the elevator up to the second floor. When she pushed open the door to Dr. Slikowski's office, she had every intention of seeking advice from him, and from Dyson as well. Free-form jazz with a lot of horns—more traditional than Slick's usual fare—was playing in the office as she entered.

The M.E. sat in his wheelchair next to Dyson's desk. Dyson was hunched over his computer. Behind them, Danny and Audrey gazed intently at the computer screen. None of them even registered Jenna's entering, which gave her a second to compose herself. At the moment Danny was the person she wanted to talk to most, and the person she wanted to see the least. He'd put himself out for her, but he was also on the other side of this case as far as she was concerned.

"Hello," she ventured, trying to keep her expression as neutral as possible.

When Dr. Slikowski saw her, he broke into a broad, uncharacteristic smile.

"Ah, Jenna," he said, "there you are. Perfect timing. I was just telling everyone how our conversation yesterday led to the hypothesis that the killer was eating the hearts for some imagined nutritional benefit."

"Uh-huh," Jenna replied. "Pretty stupid, huh?"

"Not at all," Slick said, slightly taken aback. "In

fact, after you discovered that all the victims had the same blood type, it was a matter of a bit of research to discover that wasn't all they had in common. No, actually, it looks like we were right."

Jenna stared at him. "What?"

"Yeah, that's what I said at first," Dyson threw in, grinning. "But not only can we guess why he's choosing his victims—unless this is the biggest damn coincidence in the world—we think we've figured out *how* he's choosing them as well."

Jenna didn't know what to say. "That's . . . great," she managed.

"Great doesn't cover it," Danny said.

Slick beamed proudly. "We make quite a team, Jenna. Quite a team."

She knew she ought to have been thrilled, both with the news and with the fact that Slick was so pleased with her. But Jenna couldn't think about those things. All she could think about was the fact that they finally had a lead, that they'd probably know the truth soon.

And she wasn't sure she wanted to know the answer.

"Well?" Jenna said, looking around the office at them. "Does anyone want to let me in on it?"

Danny took a breath as if he were about to say something, but Audrey shot him a hard look, and he shut up quickly. Jenna frowned. Neither detective said anything. Jenna filed that away for later: if Audrey had some problem with her, she'd like to know what it was.

Dr. Slikowski spoke up. "They all have the same insurance carrier," he explained. "Which makes it likely that someone is using that carrier's computer database to sift around for victims."

"Yeah, but that could be anyone. I mean, any competent hacker could crack those files if they wanted to," Jenna explained. "Yoshiko could do it quicker than I could microwave popcorn."

"So she's a suspect then," Dyson joked.

"Not funny," Jenna told him.

"You're right, of course," Audrey said. "But we're betting it's simpler than that. Why, specifically, do they all come from this one carrier? If it was a hacker, the killer could cover his tracks better by hacking into several different insurance companies."

"It's more likely to be someone who has access to that information," Danny explained, not meeting her eyes.

"Of course, that could be any number of people. Doctors, nurses, administrators, sales personnel," Dr. Slikowski noted. "But we all agree it stands to reason that the killer is likely to have the same blood type as his victims. That narrows the search down considerably."

"Well," Danny hedged. "It gives us a place to start, at least."

Jenna nodded. It was all making sense to her now. A sick kind of sense. But she had to admit that it felt good knowing that she had been a part of the process that had gotten them this far. If they brought the killer down, it would be partly because she and Slick had been working on the case.

"So what now?" she asked.

They all looked at her oddly.

After a moment Audrey zipped up her jacket. "Now," she said, "Danny and I go and find the guy."

Jenna frowned. "Well, *yeah*," she said. "But

you're going to need help, right? With computer files, medical records. To narrow down your suspects. We can help with that. I mean, we're all in this together. The guy isn't exactly caught yet. I may not know much more about police work than I've seen on television, but I know about puzzles. A puzzle isn't done until the last piece is snapped into place."

She looked to Dyson for support, but he glanced away.

Slick wheeled back from the desk slightly, and then pushed himself forward until he was right in front of her.

"Our job is through, Jenna," he said. "We've done all that we can and it's up to the police now. Time for the detectives to take what we've given them and bring the killer to ground."

Jenna blinked. Glanced around at them. Danny didn't look away, and she was oddly glad of that.

"That's it? I'm just supposed to go about my business now, right? Nothing to see here, citizen? Knowing the guy's out there, and you guys are closing in."

"That's about it, yes," Audrey Gaines said distantly. "We appreciate what you've done, but if I'm not mistaken, Dr. Slikowski has other cases to work on."

Jenna looked at Slick, who nodded.

"We've got one in the cold room now," he confirmed. "Drowned in the Charles. The family is apparently claiming that if the river weren't so polluted, he might have lived long enough to reach the bank, pull himself out."

She looked at each of them in turn. "All right," she said, slipping off her jacket and throwing it over the back of her chair. "Let's get to work."

A few minutes later the M.E. had said his goodbyes to the detectives, who went out in relative silence. Danny glanced back on his way out the door, and she offered him a halfhearted smile.

By the time Jenna was riding the elevator down to the basement with Slick and Dyson, she had begun to feel strange. Different. *Relieved,* she thought. *That whole weight-off-the-shoulders thing.* And it was. Everything related to this case had been a nightmare. And now, her part in that nightmare was over.

It felt good.

The good feeling didn't last very long. Jenna was out of it, and that was really okay with her. She'd come much too close to a killer once before, and didn't relish the idea of doing so again. *Let the cops do their job. Fine.*

Once she was officially out of it, distanced from it, she was haunted by the knowledge that the killer was still out there. Wednesday night and most of Thursday she was depressed and anxious, unable to concentrate on her studies. The son of a bitch had murdered her best friend, might as well have torn out her own heart as well. And he was still free—getting ready to do it to somebody else, more than likely.

That thought disturbed Jenna deeply.

She was disconnected from the investigation so completely that she felt both helpless and afraid. The other result of being disconnected was that she had room in her head and heart now for the pain. That was a major contributor to her depression and anxiety: there was time to mourn.

Then there was Pierce.

Jenna figured it couldn't harm her to let him know that the police had a new avenue to pursue, although she thought it better to keep the details to herself. The last thing she wanted was for Pierce to get himself any deeper into this thing.

They met at the Campus Center for dinner, and though the conversation was something Jenna felt should be private, she felt better with the throng of students around her. In some ways it was just as private as if they'd been alone because there were so many people that they were anonymous.

Pierce was her brother. Someone they'd both cared for was dead. When the killer had finally been brought to justice, Pierce would still be her brother. Life would go on. Jenna needed to connect with that and find common ground with him.

"I'm sorry" was the first thing she said when they sat down.

The second thing was "Pass the salt."

Pierce smiled at that. "I was pretty pissed at you," he said as he handed over the plastic shaker.

Jenna shook some over her French fries. "I don't blame you," she said. "But don't think you're off the hook that easily. You've been crawling around campus playing superhero for days, and that's not helping anyone."

His smile disappeared, and Pierce's expression was cold.

"See!" she snapped. "That's just what I mean. You're not a cop, Pierce. This is their job, not yours. If you have information that can help the case, fine, but just because you have certain training, don't think you can take the law into your own hands. You'll end up getting killed if you put yourself in the middle."

Pierce took a deep breath. Her words were reaching him, Jenna could see that. She was glad. She didn't want anything to happen to Pierce. It wasn't that she thought she needed to make it up to him for not having been one hundred percent convinced of his innocence. He had his own sins to repent. But they had to move on.

"So, how long did they hold you Tuesday?" she asked, changing the subject.

"I didn't get home until almost two in the morning," Pierce told her. "Detective Gaines gave me the don't-leave-town speech. I'm sure they'll grab me again the second they find an opportunity. Until they have a better suspect, they've pretty much decided it's me."

Jenna shook her head, frowning. "Not anymore."

Pierce looked up, eyebrows raised. "What do you mean?"

"They have a new lead. I doubt you're even a suspect anymore."

"Could have fooled me," Pierce said. "When I left this morning, I had a police tail on me."

"How could you tell?" Jenna asked.

He glanced at her as if she were an idiot. "It's my job."

Jenna let that stew for a while. They talked about their father a little, and about Jenna's mother, and made plans to go out for dinner the following week.

But Jenna was still working on a problem that was nagging at her. Pierce shouldn't be a suspect anymore. Sure, they had to keep him on the list, but to have surveillance on him seemed a bit much.

Fine, he's still a suspect, she thought after a while. *I can fix that.*

"Pierce?" she said through a mouthful of French fries slathered in ketchup. "Do you know your blood type?"

His eyes narrowed with suspicion. "Why?"

"I think I can get the cops off your back," she said. "If you trust me."

There was a moment of awkward silence before Pierce said, "You're my little sister. Of course I trust you. But actually, I don't know my blood type. I

212

think it's, like, B positive or something, but that's from one of those high school bio lab tests, and . . . hell, I don't remember."

"Are you sure?" Jenna asked.

Pierce looked at her intently. "Do you know *your* blood type?"

Jenna thought a moment. "No," she admitted guiltily.

Pierce threw up his hands and leaned back in his chair. The conversation went back to more mundane things, but Jenna continued to work on the problem of Pierce's being cleared. She was determined now to locate the information she needed to get the police to leave him alone.

Thursday night was uneventful, with one exception. Hunter had called to confirm that he would be returning to school the next day. It meant Jenna would have to miss international relations, but it was more important that she and Yoshiko be at the airport to pick him up.

She also asked him what his blood type was.

Since he hadn't been around for the most recent murder, the police no longer considered Hunter a suspect. But that didn't mean he wasn't a potential target. Fortunately, he didn't have the same blood type as his sister. Jenna was relieved. Hunter had suffered enough.

★　★　★

On Friday morning she called Slick's office to say she wouldn't be in that day. Dyson answered, and after she explained herself, and he told her it wouldn't be a problem, she asked if he'd heard anything about the heart thief case.

He had, but couldn't discuss it.

"But this is me you're talking to, Dyson," Jenna said.

Dyson confided in her that the police had narrowed their list of suspects down and had a primary suspect. A salesman for SCHP named Jarrod Coffey.

Jarrod Coffey. So now he has a name. Wonder how they narrowed it down? I'll have to ask Danny . . . if I ever speak to him again.

That had been Jenna's thought when Dyson told her about it, but later, while she was driving her dad's car to the airport with Yoshiko, she realized she'd jumped to conclusions. As far as she knew, this Coffey was just another suspect. Just like Pierce. And Pierce was innocent.

Until they know they've got the right guy, I'm not convicting anyone.

It was warm for October, nearly seventy, and Jenna had her window open as she turned off Interstate 93 and waited in traffic to get through the Callahan Tunnel to Logan Airport.

"I'm sort of nervous," Yoshiko admitted to Jenna as they entered the tunnel.

Jenna glanced quickly at her, then looked back at

the brake lights of the car in front of her. It was stop and go through the tunnel.

"You don't know what to say to Hunter?"

"No clue," Yoshiko admitted.

"Me either," Jenna told her.

Ten minutes later they pulled into the crowded short-term parking lot at Logan, got out, and went into the terminal. They waited beyond a security checkpoint with the other people who were there to pick up friends and family.

Passengers emerged from the checkpoint in spurts as planes disgorged their human cargo. After nearly twenty minutes of waiting, Yoshiko perked up.

"There he is," she said, her voice low.

Jenna saw him then. Hunter looked, if possible, thinner than when he left. His blond hair had been cut shorter than usual, almost a buzz cut. He spotted them, and a broad grin stretched across his face as he raised an arm and waved wildly. Jenna and Yoshiko both smiled back, and moved forward.

"God, am I glad to see y'all," Hunter said, and his relief sounded very real. "I believe I've decided I don't like flying very much."

His accent was stronger than when he'd left, reflecting the time he'd spent at home with his mother and other relatives.

"I'm glad you're back," Jenna told him, and pulled Hunter into an embrace. He dropped his bags and hugged her back.

"Good to see you, Jenna," he said. "I was worried about you."

Jenna laughed, stepping back from him. "*You* were worried about *me*?"

" 'Course I was," Hunter said, almost hurt. "I had my mom, my family around. You didn't. Then I realized that you had Yoshiko, so I didn't worry anymore."

Yoshiko stared at the floor, embarassed, as Hunter turned to face her.

"You're not gonna give me a hug?" he asked, opening his arms.

She went to him then, and Hunter and Yoshiko embraced for a long time. Jenna smiled to herself a little. There was more to their hug than just friends reuniting. She wondered if Hunter was aware of it. Certainly Yoshiko was. From where she stood, Jenna could see the expression on Yoshiko's face.

Bliss was the only word to describe her face.

Then Yoshiko pulled away to look up at Hunter.

"So you're back," Yoshiko said. "Are you *back*, back?"

Hunter smiled. Jenna thought it was kind of a sad smile. Then Hunter reached out and took Yoshiko's hand.

"I think so," he said. Hunter looked at Jenna, and reached for her hand as well. "Thank you both for coming," he said and they went down to baggage claim to get his luggage; then the three of them walked out to the car.

It felt good and right having him back, but Jenna knew that things couldn't begin to return to normal until Melody's killer had been caught.

They celebrated Hunter's return in an appropriately reserved fashion by hanging out in Jenna and Yoshiko's room, watching sitcoms and talking. Hunter, pretty tired, went back to his room before ten.

After he'd gone, Jenna sat down to read a bit and Yoshiko got her e-mail and did some research for the fundamentals of law class she was taking. Jenna's father was her professor, and Jenna always made sure to tease Yoshiko about not expecting favoritism.

Jenna was barely able to keep her eyes on the page of the book she was reading. It was a fascinating novel called *The Anubis Gates*, about English professors and time travel. *Fascinating, yep. So why can't I focus?*

The answer to that one was simple: Pierce. It was bugging Jenna that the cops were still watching him. Really getting under her skin. So much so, that she was even more determined to eliminate him as a suspect. The police obviously weren't willing to do so, even though they had every reason to scratch him off their list.

Unable to concentrate, Jenna glanced over at Yoshiko. The girl's fingers tapped rapidly on her keyboard. Her profile was framed in the light from the screen. She didn't spend her whole life in front of the computer; Yoshiko had too much interest in learning and life for that. But she was a natural-born hacker, no question. It was just the way her mind worked.

Jenna thought it pretty ironic, actually. All that hacking was sort of like solving puzzles, which she loved and was good at. But hacking, or even successfully navigating the Internet, didn't come easily to her.

"Hey, Yoshiko," Jenna said.

The other girl typed another couple of words, then turned in her chair. Jenna explained quickly what was on her mind. Then she got to the question.

"What?" Yoshiko cried, staring at Jenna as though she were insane. "No. Uh-uh. Even if I could hack the medical records of the Marine Corps, I wouldn't do it. Okay, I mean, I might be able to do it . . . but no way, Jenna. The other stuff I've done for you was simple, but now you're talking jail time."

Jenna chewed her lower lip, eyes downcast. "I know. I'm sorry."

"Me, too," Yoshiko said.

She went back to her research, while Jenna kept playing with the puzzle in her mind. There had to be a way to get Pierce's medical records, or something close to them. A blood type was like a fingerprint, it was never going to change. Which meant that old records would still be accurate.

And before Pierce joined the Corps, he'd lived with his father. Jenna's father. *Here in Somerset.*

"Hey," Jenna said hopefully.

"What now?" Yoshiko asked. "You want me to hack the White House computer?"

Jenna shot her a hard look. "Wiseass. I want you to hack Somerset Community Health Plan's patient files."

Yoshiko's brow furrowed. After a few seconds, she said, "Okay. I guess I can do that."

It was past eleven o'clock when Yoshiko sat back and looked at Jenna in triumph.

"Logan, Pierce F.," she said happily. "His records are still here."

Jenna was ecstatic. "This is so cool!" she cried. "Now we can clear him. Pierce is going to be so psyched. Can you print that?"

Yoshiko clicked on the Print icon and the laser printer started to hum. Jenna was reading the information on the screen over Yoshiko's shoulder. Pierce had a scar on his left bicep, which she'd never noticed. Her eyes moved over the records, including height, weight, eye color.

Blood type.

Jenna gasped in surprise.

"Oh my God."

chapter 14

"This is not good," Yoshiko muttered. "It doesn't prove anything, but God, I mean, the odds of Pierce's having this blood type are out of the ballpark, y'know?"

Jenna shook her head. She was grim, but calm. "Not really," she said. "No more so than Melody's having it. I guess the odds of them both having it are high, but not impossible."

Her mind was spinning, and she sat down hard on the floor and leaned against the footboard of her bed.

"It all makes so much more sense now," she said, more to herself than Yoshiko. "I mean, no wonder the police never took him off their list of suspects. But the police weren't about to let me in on the secret."

Yoshiko crouched down beside her and reached for her hand. "No, Jenna," she said. "Don't go there. Besides, it doesn't make sense. I mean, how would Pierce have gotten access to those records to figure out who the potential victims were?"

Jenna stared at her.

"Okay, I could do it," Yoshiko admitted. "But I don't remember Pierce ever showing the slightest interest in computers, never mind letting slip that he's a hacker."

"Why would he?" Jenna argued.

Yoshiko didn't have an answer for that. Jenna picked up the phone and began to dial. She listened as it rang several times, and then an answering machine picked up. Then the machine was disconnected, and a sleepy voice said, "Hello?"

"Dad, it's Jenna," she said quickly.

"Jenna? What's going on?" her father asked anxiously. *With all that's happening with the murders, and Pierce as a suspect, he's got every reason to be anxious,* Jenna thought.

Especially now.

As quickly as she could, Jenna explained the situation.

"I hear you, but from the tone of your voice, it doesn't sound like you think Pierce is . . . behind all this," her father said.

"I guess I don't," Jenna replied. "But maybe I just don't want to. We can't be too careful. Look,

I'm coming over there now, and I think you and I should sit and talk to Pierce together."

It was all working itself out in her head. Even if Pierce had been doing all of this, if she and her father confronted him together, surely he wouldn't try anything. And if he did, well, there were two of them.

But it isn't him, she told herself. *No way.*

"Are you listening, Jenna?"

"No, sorry, Dad, I kind of spaced out. What was that?"

"Pierce isn't here," Frank informed her. "He hasn't been around all day. So you can save yourself a trip, at least for tonight. I'll expect you first thing in the morning, say, nine?"

Jenna thought about it. But her father was right, there was no reason to go and wait for him; no telling what time he might come in.

"All right," she replied.

"Just one thing," he went on. "You should know that this afternoon, someone broke into my apartment."

"What?"

"Split the frame and broke the lock on the front door in broad daylight," Frank confirmed. "The damnedest thing. And strangest of all, as far as I can tell, they didn't take anything. Nothing."

"Did you fix the lock?"

"Taken care of," Frank replied.

"Please be careful. Put the chain on. If Pierce

comes home, he can knock to wake you. I have no idea what's going on, but none of it's good."

Frank agreed. Father and daughter said their good-byes and Jenna hung up. When she turned around, Yoshiko was staring at her.

"He's not home?" Yoshiko asked.

"No. And I'm not sure I want to know where he is," Jenna confessed.

Pierce Logan stood among the trees across Alfe Street from the Alpha Omicron Pi sorority house. From there, he had an excellent view of two sides of the house and could see the roof fairly well.

He watched and waited for an opportunity to present itself.

It was cold, and his dark leather jacket was not warm enough, but he barely shivered. In counter-intelligence training, Pierce had been through far worse than this. Standing there in the cold, leaning against a tree, sucking on a cherry LifeSaver—this was luxurious by comparison.

A car turned from Carpenter onto Alfe, and Pierce stood rigid, as he always did when a car moved past. Rapid movement could give him away, and he didn't want to have to explain his presence here again. He couldn't afford any time away from his post. When the opportunity presented itself, when the target presented itself, he wanted to be ready.

The car slowed as it began to move down Alfe. Tires crunched debris on the street. Pierce frowned as the car moved up parallel with his position, and then simply stopped. He could hear the sound of the transmission being ratcheted into Park, and still he only stared. To bolt now would give his position away, and if it had already been compromised, running would only make things worse.

The engine ceased to rumble, and it ticked down a few times. The driver's door opened, and Pierce smiled thinly as Danny Mariano climbed out. Danny walked around the car and over to the edge of the road, staring into the trees. Eyes focusing. Staring right at Pierce.

"I drove by twice already, trying to figure out exactly where you were," Danny told him. "Figured it was a bit less conspicuous than using the spotlight."

"True," Pierce agreed, still deep in the trees.

"Are you coming out, or do I have to come in after you?"

Pierce made his way through the trees to the edge of the street. A moment later, he and Danny were standing face-to-face. The two men sized each other up, but Pierce said nothing.

"What are you doing here, Pierce?"

"You must have some idea about that, Detective, or you wouldn't have known where to look for me."

"We've had several reports of a man lurking around here. Plus, I picked you up here the other night, remember?"

Pierce shook his head. "That's not it, and you know it."

"I suppose you're going to tell me you didn't know that Maggie March, an AOPi sister, has the same blood type as the other victims," the detective said.

Pierce narrowed his eyes. "Actually, that explains a lot. But no, I didn't know that."

"Kind of figured you'd say that. I'm trying to figure out why I believe you," Danny said, shaking his head.

"You shouldn't believe me, Detective. It's your job to be skeptical. Of course, I'm glad you do," Pierce admitted.

Danny took a breath, let it out, and then studied Pierce's face for a moment. "Did you know your father's apartment was broken into today?" he asked.

"No. I didn't."

"Do you have your keys to his place?"

Pierce drew them out and dangled them, jangling, in front of the detective's face. "Is my father all right?"

"He wasn't home at the time and it doesn't seem like anything was taken."

"That's strange," Pierce said, still trying to figure out what Mariano was up to. "Are you sure?"

"Nope. But it has me wondering."

Pierce just waited for him to continue, knowing that he would.

"You're a good suspect," Danny went on. "No real alibi. Motive in at least one case. Pretty damn bizarre behavior. And the same blood type as all the victims, which the M.E. and our psych consultant at the FBI have agreed the perp probably has. You've also got the training to get in and out, elude capture, all that crap."

With a slight chuckle, Pierce shook his head. "Oh, right. I've done such an excellent job eluding capture so far."

Danny narrowed his eyes. "But you could if you wanted to, couldn't you?"

Pierce nodded.

"See, I don't know why I get the feeling you're not the guy, but when I talk to you, the feeling goes away pretty fast," the detective said. "Between your training and your attitude, you do make one hell of a suspect."

A car went by, headlights bathing both men in their illumination for a moment. Several students crossed Carpenter Street headed for the AOPi house. It was about twenty minutes to midnight.

"So," Pierce said. "What are you going to do?"

Danny didn't respond at first, but from the way his eyes danced around, Pierce knew the detective was holding something back.

"What've you got? You're not sharing all this with me just because you decided that I didn't do it," he said.

As though he'd just made a decision, Danny said,

"You're right. There's something that's been bothering me. I don't know how much of this your sister has told you, but all the victims have the same blood type, and the same insurance carrier. It's the same carrier your father uses, and you were on his policy until about six years ago. Thing is, you showed up on the computer records, your entire medical history up to that time six years ago."

"Maybe I'm shooting myself in the foot here, but what's odd about that?"

"The only records available in the database we accessed are active ones. Yours shouldn't have been there," Mariano admitted.

Pierce frowned. "So somebody added my file to that database," he said, piecing it together. "Maybe even changed my blood type to match the victims'."

"Yep," Mariano replied. "And recently."

"So there's someone out there other than you who wants me to take the fall for these killings," Pierce said, staring at the detective. "Of course, it could be a fluke. Maybe I want it to look like that. Maybe I am the guy after all. That's what's in your head, isn't it? You just can't be sure."

"No, I can't be. Thing is, if someone's trying to set you up, he hasn't convinced anyone yet. And the killer wouldn't be off the hook unless the frame job was conclusive. Already it's started to unravel. A lot of people are fighting to clear you, including your sister, and she can be damned persuasive."

The fire in Pierce's gut was replaced by a solid

block of ice. The chill ran up his spine and spread through his entire body. An idea was starting to form, and it terrified him.

"Be nice for the heart thief to have us both out of the way, wouldn't it?" he said.

Mariano's eyes widened. "Are you suggesting . . ."

"What better way to set me up than to kill my sister, who, let's agree, has been poking her nose a little too deeply into this thing? Somebody broke into my father's house. Who's to say something wasn't stolen? Maybe something meant to be incriminating."

Danny wasn't listening—he was already rushing around to the driver's side of his car.

"Get in!" he snapped.

As he climbed into the car, Pierce could hear his own heart beat. His pulse had begun to race.

Jenna, he thought grimly, staring out the window as the car reversed direction then tore wildly up Carpenter Street.

"Jenna, you're not going to be any good to anyone in the morning if you don't get some sleep."

There was an old horror movie called *The Devil Rides Out* on TNT. Jenna was only watching because she knew it was written by the legendary Richard Matheson, but it had turned out to be nice and creepy. What little of it she had been able to concentrate on. She hadn't actually been able to focus on much in the past hour or so as she lay on the floor and stared at the flickering television.

Now she glanced up at Yoshiko, who hung her head over the edge of her top bunk and stared down at Jenna.

"Unless you're sleeping with your eyes open," Yoshiko added.

Jenna offered a tired smile. "Nope. Just a little preoccupied."

"I don't blame you," Yoshiko replied. "But, look, why don't you go to bed? The sooner you fall asleep, the sooner the morning comes."

Nodding in agreement, or surrender, Jenna dragged herself to her feet, then pulled her robe over her flannel nightshirt. "I think I need to take a shower to relax. I'll be back. I'll try to be quiet. No reason to keep you up just because I can't sleep."

"Oh, now you decide to be nice to me," Yoshiko teased. Then she rolled over, fluffed her pillow under her head, and sighed deeply.

Jenna watched her a moment, then pulled a towel from her closet and picked up the wire basket she kept all her toiletries in. She could brush her teeth or wash her face at the sink in their room, but anything more complicated required a trip down the hall, which meant lugging all her stuff down there. The wire basket had been a gift from her mother, and it came in handy every day.

She closed the door quietly behind her. Off toward the boys' side, in the common area, a girl lay draped across a chair reading from a textbook while a small group of kids were playing a game of quarters. How long they'd been playing was made clear by their obvious drunkenness. Jenna paid them no attention. That was dorm life. She just hoped none of them threw up out there, or the smell would last for days.

Jenna turned away and started down the hall toward the bathroom.

Danny jerked the steering wheel to the right and took a sharp turn into the faculty parking lot behind Sparrow Hall. His mind was whirling with possibilities, but he wasn't convinced they were more than that. Nothing made total sense. He didn't really believe Pierce Logan was responsible for the murders, and there was a certain logic in Pierce's suggestion that Jenna could be in trouble.

If there was another killer, and Pierce was getting too close, killing Jenna and framing Pierce would indeed kill two birds with one vicious stone.

Danny found that the concept of Jenna in danger terrified him. No matter what kind of age difference there was between them, and though he'd never pursue a relationship with her, Danny couldn't lie to himself. He cared for Jenna, and he wasn't about to let her be hurt.

When Danny slammed on the brakes and threw the car into Park, Pierce was out of the car instantly. Danny yanked out the keys and slipped them into his pocket as he jumped out. He ran around the car, staring up at the windows. Jenna's room was back here somewhere, but he couldn't see anything odd.

"Let's move!" Pierce snapped as he went around the side of the building and headed for the front entrance.

Danny hustled to catch up. He started to sprint and rounded the side of Sparrow Hall at a good clip. The last thing he expected to see was Pierce Logan standing there blocking him. He had barely an eyeblink to respond, and all Danny could do was begin to form a question.

Pierce's fist flew out and shattered Danny's nose, and the detective crumbled to the ground. He was disoriented as Pierce leaned over him. Danny tried to struggle as Pierce choked off his air with one powerful hand on his throat. With the other, Pierce drove a thumb into a pressure point at his neck. Danny felt himself slipping away, saw nothing but blackness.

When Pierce hit him again, he barely felt it.

Then he was unconscious.

Jenna was letting the hot water from the shower pound against her shoulder blades. The heat was working, relaxing her muscles, easing the tension out of her back and neck and shoulders. Her eyes were closed, and she could feel the urge to sleep creeping over her gradually. It felt good.

She turned and let the hot water stream down her face.

The bathroom door whined as someone came in. Jenna barely noticed as she turned off the water. She squeezed as much water as she could from her hair, and reached over the glass door to grab her towel from the outer stall. Jenna toweled dry quickly and then stepped onto the tile floor of the outer stall. The metal door separating her from the rest of the bathroom had profanity scrawled across it, but also some very sweet poetry, and several very amusing jokes. She'd read them all before, but her eyes swept over them again as she wrapped the towel around her hair and slipped into her robe.

She sat down on the small wooden bench in the outer stall and reached down to the wire basket. There were things in there she wouldn't need tonight . . . deodorant, body mist, hair gel; she wasn't going anywhere except to sleep . . . but the essentials were there: her brush, blow-dryer, body lotion.

While she was rubbing the lotion on her feet, Jenna stopped suddenly, and paused, cocking her head to one side. She recalled having heard the door open, but she hadn't heard a single sound since then. Not the toilet flushing, not the sink or shower running.

Puzzled, Jenna pulled on her slippers, stood and pulled her robe more tightly around her.

"Hello?" she said out loud. "Is anyone there?"

No response. Feeling rather silly, Jenna stood on the bench and tried to peer over the gap at the top of the stall, but she couldn't see much more than the top of the long mirror on the other side of the bathroom. She frowned, stepped down, and un-latched the metal stall door.

"Hello?" she said again, more tentatively now.

He was smiling at her.

"Hello," he said in reply.

The man in the raincoat was very ordinary look-ing, with curly brown hair and wide blue eyes. Jenna saw the scalpel in his hand, and she screamed.

Then he lunged for her, his left hand grabbing her by the shoulder and his right thrusting the scal-pel into the stall, the door slamming open against the tile wall. Jenna didn't think twice about it; she spun back, out of his reach, then grabbed the metal door and whipped it closed again, throwing all of her weight behind it and forcing him backward. She kept screaming, hoping someone would hear and come to help. Even the drunken goofballs playing quarters in the common area.

His right hand, the scalpel in his grip, was caught between the door and the frame, and he cried out in pain. Jenna felt adrenaline humming through her body as she slammed against the door again, hoping to break his arm, or at least make him drop the blade.

No such luck.

"Damn it!" she snapped, as he pulled his hand free, with the scalpel still in his grip.

She slid the lock into place just as he kicked at the door. It wouldn't be long, she knew. Not long at all. A second or two, that was all. He kicked the door again, and Jenna knew she needed to do something to throw him off.

"I know who you are!" she screamed. "And so will everyone in this building in a second. Jarrod Coffey! That's your name. Jarrod Coffey!"

It was a chance, she knew. It might not be Coffey at all. He was the number one suspect, according to what she'd heard, but that didn't mean it was him.

There was a pause in his attack on the door—a bit of quiet. Jenna screamed his name again.

"Shut up, you bitch!" he hissed. So it was Coffey after all.

Jenna was beginning to lose hope that someone would hear her. Most everyone was asleep or drunk, and anyone woken by her screaming would probably pass it off as someone having a fight or something, and be more pissed off than concerned.

No, she had to assume she was on her own.

The door was kicked again, and the thin metal around the latch began to pull away. Glancing around, Jenna reached down and picked up the wire basket and opened the glass door behind her. She stepped into the still-wet shower stall, dropping the basket and grabbing for its contents with both hands.

With the next kick, the metal door slammed inward, hit the still-open shower door, and the glass shattered, raining down onto the tile floor of the outer stall.

"I don't have time for this," Coffey said, snarling as he brandished the scalpel, glass crunching under his boots as he came for her.

Jenna lifted the bottle of body mist in her right hand and pushed the button on top, sending a stream of it directly into Coffey's eyes. He screamed and reached for his face with his left hand, blinking, trying to keep his eyes open despite the pain. He still held the scalpel, but he was stumbling back a bit.

"I can't see, damn you. You can't do this."

Dropping the bottle, Jenna wound the coiled cord of her blow-dryer around her fist. Then she moved in and swung the big chunk of plastic and metal over her head as hard as she could. It connected with Coffey's forehead, with a loud crack of splintering plastic.

The man shrieked in pain and backpedaled, moving out of the stall, still unable to see. He held his hands up to protect himself, still holding the scalpel.

"Drop that thing!" Jenna shouted.

He tensed at the sound of her voice, trying to blink away the pain in his eyes. Using her voice to locate her, he thrust out with the scalpel.

Jenna brought the blow-dryer down again. It was split open already, and this time the metal grill cut a ragged gash down the side of Coffey's face. He stumbled back a little farther, and went down on his knees, using a sink to keep himself from going down completely.

But he dropped the scalpel.

The door was just past him. Jenna could reach it. Get help. It was all over now.

Thank God.

She rushed for the door, just as it swung open and Pierce barreled in, face etched with rage and hate. He took one look at her, then he looked past her to where Coffey was just pulling himself to his feet. And Pierce smiled.

Jenna didn't like that smile.

Pierce pushed past her, grabbed Coffey by the back of his raincoat collar, and drove the man's face into the huge mirror, which cracked into a vast, reflective spiderweb design.

Then he did it again.

"Pierce, God, stop it!" Jenna screamed.

He turned toward her, face flushed red with his fury, eyes slitted.

"He killed Melody. He was going to kill you. There's no death penalty in this state, Jenna. If they take him in, he'll probably end up in goddamn therapy. This is the only way for him to pay."

With a loud grunt, Pierce slammed Coffey's skull off the sink, crushing his nose. Blood spurted across the white porcelain, and then the man crumpled down to the cold tile below. Pierce hauled back a leg and kicked Coffey in the side. Jenna was certain she heard something snap and realized Pierce had broken at least one of the killer's ribs.

The killer. Coffey, yeah. But in a second, that's gonna be Pierce too.

She had to stop him.

"Pierce, I said no!" she snapped, and ran at him, feeling ridiculous in her robe and slippers, trying to hold the fleece tight around her.

Jenna grabbed Pierce's arm to pull him away, and he clutched her by the throat and slammed her against the metal wall between the shower stall doors.

"Don't do that again," he said dangerously.

Releasing her, Pierce crouched down and grabbed Coffey's head. With powerful arms, he hefted the man up. He wound one arm around the heart thief's throat, and Jenna knew what was coming. Pierce would break his neck. She closed her eyes. She didn't want to see it.

The bathroom door slammed open, clacking against the wall, shattering a tile. Jenna opened her eyes to see Danny Mariano standing in the open door, nose mashed and bleeding, his gun gripped in both hands, aimed directly at Pierce.

"Let him go!" Danny shouted. "Now!"

Jenna looked past him and saw that there were a bunch of people crowded in the hall now. People who'd heard some kind of commotion but were afraid to come in. In that split second, though, she saw Yoshiko, Hunter, and Damon Harris, all pushing through the crowd.

"Get back!" Danny snapped at them. Then he returned his attention to Pierce.

For his part, Pierce only glared at Danny, his arm still around Coffey's throat.

"You still think I'm the heart thief, Detective? I've got your man right here. Why don't you wait outside while I finish this the way it has to end? Save us all a whole lot of trouble and heartache."

Danny took two steps forward, weapon still trained on Pierce. "Put the man down now, Lieutenant. You're under arrest. More than likely, you'll be able to talk your way out of it, considering the circumstances. But if I have to put a bullet in you, that's a whole different story."

Pierce hesitated.

"Now!" Danny roared.

For an eyeblink, Jenna thought Pierce was going to snap Coffey's neck. His muscles seemed tensed to do it, but then all of a sudden, he relaxed, and let the man slip to the tile, his face a bloody mess.

"I should've hit you harder," Pierce said to the detective.

Danny kept his weapon trained on Pierce and walked around behind him. "You have the right to remain silent . . ."

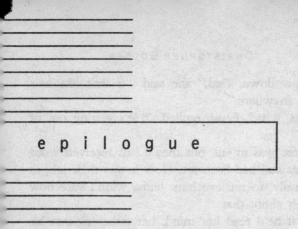

epilogue

Yoshiko and Hunter sat up with her for hours. Shortly before dawn, Jenna finally drifted off to sleep.

When she woke Saturday morning, at a quarter past ten, Yoshiko and Hunter lay together, fully clothed, on the top bunk, huddled together in a tight embrace. Jenna threw a blanket over them.

Just after one o'clock, Jenna's father picked her up in front of Somerset Medical Center. She'd been to visit Dr. Slikowski, and now she had an even more important errand to run—one which filled her with a great many conflicting feelings.

She ran to the car and opened the door, then slid into the passenger seat and slammed her door shut. Her father had begun to accelerate even before she buckled her seat belt.

"Slow down, Dad," she said. "It isn't like he's going anywhere."

"Yes, it is," Frank replied. "He's getting out of there."

Pierce was in jail, but they'd just received word that his bail had been set. Now it was their job, as his family, to retrieve him. Jenna wasn't sure how she felt about that.

As if he'd read her mind, her father cleared his throat. "Why so quiet now, Jenna?"

"I'm worried about Pierce," she confessed. "I . . . you didn't see him, Dad. He needs help."

"You can't blame him for losing control, Jenna," Frank insisted. "Not after what Jarrod Coffey did to Melody and almost did to you. If Pierce hadn't come along—"

"Nothing," Jenna interrupted. "I had Coffey down. I was almost out the door. Pierce came in there to kill him, that's all there is to it."

Frank fell silent after that. Jenna didn't have anything else to say either. They rode quietly for a mile or so, until Frank glanced over at her, his expression troubled.

"What did Dr. Slikowski have to say?" he asked at length.

Jenna looked at him, knew there was more to be said, but thought better of it. "Looks like we were more right than we knew," she answered. "Coffey has the same blood type, but he also has porphyria. It's a pretty rare blood disorder that causes a kind of malfunction in which the body stops breaking hemoglobin down the right way."

"Say that in English," Frank suggested.

"Think of it like this," Jenna said. "Your blood cells die, and new ones replace them. But if you can't get rid of the old ones, the system starts to go all wonky."

"Wonky? Is that English?"

"You get the idea," Jenna said sternly. "Thing is, the porphyria made Coffey get all crazy, and he started to think that he needed to replenish his blood, and his energy, using other people's blood. Dyson says the guy actually thought eating the hearts would somehow fix his condition. The fact that he had such a rare blood type just made him work harder to choose his victims, and . . ."

Her voice trailed off. Frank glanced over at her. "Thinking about Melody?"

"Actually, about Pierce," she admitted. "He was right, in a way. Coffey is recovering. But given his medical condition and the fact that he's obviously a nutjob, he'll probably end up in some psychiatric treatment center for the rest of his life."

She paused and looked out the window, not wanting to see her father's face.

"It scares me to think he won't be held account-able. But you know what scares me more, Dad? The idea that if Pierce walks away, he won't really understand that what he did was wrong. He needs counseling. You have to be the one to make sure he gets it."

Frank braked and flicked on the signal to turn into the police station parking lot. He glanced over at Jenna.

"What can I do?" he asked, clearly troubled.

"You're his father," she said. "If you talk to him about this, I think he'll listen."

When Pierce was brought out to them, Frank pulled him close and hugged him tightly. Jenna looked away. They were about to turn to leave when she saw Danny and Audrey Gaines coming down the corridor toward them.

"You go on ahead," she told her father and brother. "I'll be right there."

Pierce had the decency to look away as Danny came toward him. Jenna was heartened by that. At least he knew enough to realize he was in the wrong. Then he and Frank were out the door and down the stairs, and Jenna turned to face Danny and Audrey.

"Hey," Jenna said, looking at Danny, whose nose was bandaged. Her gaze ticked momentarily over to Audrey. "How are you?"

"Better than your hero here," Audrey replied.

Jenna couldn't help but notice there was something odd about her tone, but she had no idea what.

"So what happens now?" she asked.

"That's up to the D.A. and the Marine Corps,"

Danny explained. "Pierce ended up with an assault and battery charge, so if he plays his cards right, he might be okay."

Jenna frowned. They both knew Danny was running interference for Pierce. He ought to be up on attempted murder, at least. She wondered why he'd do such a thing. Then it occurred to her that maybe Danny was just human. Maybe he figured that what Pierce did, Coffey had coming.

And maybe he was right. But that wasn't up to either one of them to decide. Jenna knew the law well enough to know that much.

"What about that?" she asked, pointing toward the thick bandages on Danny's nose, and the large yellow bruise on the side of his face.

"That?" Danny asked. "Hell, Jenna, Coffey did that. You know. You were there."

Even as Danny said the words, Audrey glared at him. Her disapproval of what he was doing couldn't have been any clearer. She scowled and walked away, without even saying good-bye.

Jenna smiled and shook her head. It was all a question of degree, she realized. Not who had done the right thing, but whose sins, whose crimes, were worse. Pierce was a lieutenant in the Marine Corps. He had a whole career ahead of him that was already in jeopardy. Danny wasn't about to make it worse with a charge of assaulting a police officer. But to stretch the truth that far . . . Jenna didn't know if she was comfortable with that.

But maybe Pierce could have a second chance. She certainly wished that for him. *And, really, isn't that what Danny's trying to buy him?*

Suddenly Jenna felt very tired. She just wanted to get some rest.

"You're a good guy, Danny," she said.

Then she stepped in close to him, lifted her chin, and kissed him softly, swiftly, on the lips. Danny didn't protest.

"That's in the job description, actually," he said.

"I'll see you soon," Jenna promised as she turned toward the door.

"I'll look forward to it," Danny replied.

Outside, Pierce and Frank were waiting for her. When they saw her, Frank got in and started the car, but Pierce just stood there, watching her approach.

"Jenna," he said gently. "I wanted to say I'm sorry for—"

"Don't!" she snapped suddenly.

Pierce's eyes went wide.

"Don't say it. You want to make up for what you did? Get help. Whatever it takes, you need help. What you did last night was not okay, you got it? Not under any circumstances was it okay. And if you have moments when you start thinking it was okay, that maybe you did the right thing, I want you to remember the feeling of *my* throat in your hand when you slammed me against that wall. Anytime you start thinking maybe it was okay, you remember that.

" 'Cause there isn't going to be a day that goes by that I don't think about what it felt like to have my own brother do that to me, hurt me like that."

Pierce's mouth was hanging open, the pain in his eyes unmistakable. Jenna was glad. *If he feels guilty,* she thought, *maybe there's hope.*

"If you need me, Pierce, I'll be there. I'll talk to you. I'll support you as long as you're dealing with this. But don't even think about trying to make it go away."

"I would never do that, Jenna," he promised.

Part of her wanted so badly to hug him, to hold him and tell him how scared she had been, both of Coffey, and then of him, her own brother. But she couldn't do that, not yet. She had to learn who he was all over again before she could hold him close again.

It was going to take a while.

But they'd get there.

Turn the page for
a preview of
the next
Body of Evidence thriller

SOUL SURVIVOR

Available November 1999

It was the day before Halloween, and Bill Broderick felt invincible. With the full moon shining above, he jogged along the paved path that ran beside the Charles River, on the Cambridge side, and let the adrenaline take hold.

Bill was pumped. Not just from the run, but from the day he'd had. Before he'd finished his coffee that morning, he'd managed to get Shawna Mallette to agree to dinner Halloween night. By two o'clock, he'd scored a million-dollar client for Constellation Software. Half an hour later, the district manager had called him in to congratulate him, and to let him know that a management slot would be opening up, and he was in contention for it.

At three-thirty, afraid to give such a perfect

day any chance of blemish, Bill had told his secretary to call him on the cell phone if there was anything urgent, and had headed for his fifth-floor two-bedroom overlooking the Charles. He'd listened to messages, caught up on e-mail, and then cooked himself some blackened chicken in a cast-iron skillet. With dirty rice and roasted peppers, that was dinner.

Bill had a taste for spicy food, and he loved to cook. He only wished his stomach was as cast-iron as the pan.

After dinner, he'd made a quick call to a client in La Jolla—still early out there—and then had changed into sweats. With his portable CD player pumping Joan Osborne's early recordings through the mini headphones, he'd headed out for a run.

It was chilly, but not bad at all for the end of October. Even the breeze off the river didn't really cut through his Boston College sweatshirt. The moon was full, and it shimmered on the river. *Pretty sweet*, Bill thought. You couldn't tell how dirty the Charles was after dark.

Yeah, he felt invincible.

The blood pumped through his veins and the music thrummed in his ears and his heart beat in time with his feet on the pavement. The path wound in among the trees between river and road, and Bill reminded himself how brilliant an idea it had been to move here. The new apartment was close to Harvard Square, but right on the Charles. There was always something going on, and if it was something on the river, whether it was music or the Head of the Charles regatta, he could see it from his small balcony.

Never mind the women who studied or sunned themselves in Charles River Park on every sunny day from April to September.

Which brought Bill back to Shawna. He still couldn't quite believe that she'd agreed to dinner. They'd worked together for months, and though they'd always gotten along well, she'd blown off his advances completely. And why not? He was a notorious dog. Though he didn't talk too much about his social life around her, he did plenty of bragging around the other guys at the office. All bucking to be the alpha male, of course. But there could only ever be one alpha male in any given situation. Bill wasn't one hundred percent confident that he was it, but he was damned sure he wasn't going to let anyone else take the title without a fight.

Still, in spite of his self-inflicted reputation for not exactly being the most sensitive of guys, Shawna had actually agreed to go out with him. Bill hadn't done a great job covering up his surprise, and she'd laughed at the look on his face.

"Don't be so stunned," she'd said. "I figure

once you get past the arrogant exterior, maybe there's some raw clay that could be molded into a decent guy."

Bill had smiled. "Don't get your hopes up."

Now it was his hopes that were up.

He ran, working up a good sweat, heart working, reminding him his body was a machine. That's what he always thought about when he exercised. A machine needed tending to. He nodded in time with Joan Osborne, and wondered how right Shawna might be. Sure, he was kind of a dog. But he was always honest with women, never lied to them. He thought of himself as a pretty decent guy, in spite of the fact that he never seemed to be able to stick it out with someone past the first few months.

Time would tell . . .

Bill grunted. Started to slow. The CD was between songs, and in that moment of silence, he thought he heard something. The next song started up, slow and sultry, but he reached up and pulled the headphones off.

A woman screamed.

With a low curse under his breath, his mind working furiously, Bill left the path without hesitation. The rest of the path was well lit, but there were two lights out here, and the river water looked black as he ran toward it . . . toward the bridge that went over the Charles and into Boston, with only the full moon to guide him.

There, at the base of the bridge, far from the path, he saw her. There was an expression on the woman's face as she ran from beneath the bridge, a look of fear unlike anything Bill had seen before. He had put his own fears aside, rushing to the aid of a stranger on instinct, despite the darkness, despite the abyss of the unknown. But now, as she ran toward him, not so much running as desperately flailing, he felt the first tingle of fright begin to creep up inside him, calming the lightning reflex that had prompted him to go to her aid.

But then she was there . . .

"Oh, thank God," she huffed, throwing herself into his arms. "He's . . . oh, if you hadn't come."

If she hadn't seemed so grateful, so reliant upon him, he might have left then. Just walked away with her, helped her to the police station, something like that. Something practical. But something within him heard the plaintive tone of her voice, and he stood up a little taller. Bill was angry with the bastard who'd attacked this woman. This *beautiful* woman. He hadn't noticed that at first, but she was beautiful indeed. Dark and exotic. Perhaps forty, more than ten years his senior, she was nevertheless striking. She wore a long, crimson silk scarf around her neck.

Then she said the words.

"Please don't let him get away."

Bill looked at her, into her soulful eyes. "Don't worry," he said.

And he ran for the blackness beneath the bridge. He could hear the cars rumbling above, and the soft, swift running of the river, but from the dark before him he could hear nothing.

Though he'd been coming from the darkened path, the night seemed somehow more solid down there, out of sight of the moon. It took a moment for his eyes to adjust. The lights of the city across the river, mute witness to the scene unfolding there on the bank, were all that he had to see by. But it was enough.

Bill blinked. He wanted to make certain his brain was correctly processing what he was seeing there. On the stone foundation of the bridge, in white spraypaint that picked up the light from the city, were horrible images. *A man with the head of an elephant. A figure with four arms dancing on a corpse. An orb—perhaps the moon—but with the features of a skull.*

And on the ground . . . in a wide spot that had been cleared of the sort of debris that littered the rest of that dark space, Bill saw a shopping bag on its side. Most of its contents seemed to have been laid out there on the ground: a skull, a glass jar of what might have been sand, a long knife, and several dark objects just inside the bag.

"What the hell is this?" Bill asked himself aloud.

There was no one there to hear him. Though he hadn't heard anyone running off as he approached, the woman's attacker must have escaped out to the path on the opposite side. He'd be long gone by now. But just looking at the things he'd left behind, Bill realized just how lucky the woman had been. *Better get the police down here*, he thought. *This guy is a complete nutjob. They've gotta get him before he hurts someone.*

Bill started to back up. Though he'd heard nothing, he sensed someone behind him and began to turn. He was too late. A flash of red slipped past his eyes and then he was being strangled, his air cut off completely. He knew he had to react, to thrash, to drop to the ground—something—but in the instant of hesitation and shock, he was driven forward, headfirst, into the stone foundation of the bridge.

The impact broke his nose and cut his forehead. And he fell. He was quickly running out of air, the oblivion of unconsciousness slipping over him. He tried to force his body to rise up, but it would not obey his commands.

In the last moment of thought he had left to

him, he felt the soft, tender kiss of a woman's lips. Smelled her sweet perfume. And she spoke.

"You were so brave."

Then he knew that the thing around his neck, stealing his life, was a scarf made of crimson silk . . .

He was dead. That was good. But the face had been damaged. Still, it would be all right. It would heal, if all went well. She took a thick, black marker from the bag and on his forehead she drew a third eye, above and between the ones he had been born with.

She had to drag him, just a little, so that the light of the full moon fell across his face. With her gloved hands, she opened the jar and sprinkled ashes over his body, then threw both jar and marker into the river. She knelt by the dead man for several moments, staring into his lifeless eyes, staring into the third eye she had drawn, and willing it to open, praying that it would open.

Then she lifted the skull in both hands, and with it, she began to dance.

Look for the next
***Body of Evidence* thriller**
SOUL SURVIVOR
by Christopher Golden
Available from Pocket Books
November 1999

about the author

CHRISTOPHER GOLDEN is a novelist, journalist, and comic book writer. His novels include the vampire epics *Of Saints and Shadows*, *Angel Souls & Devil Hearts*, and *Of Masques and Martyrs*, as well as such media tie-ins as *Buffy the Vampire Slayer: Child of the Hunt* (which he co-wrote with Nancy Holder), *Hellboy: The Lost Army*, and the current hardcover *X-Men: Codename Wolverine*. He is one of the authors of the recently released book *The Watcher's Guide: The Official Companion to Buffy the Vampire Slayer*.

Golden's comic book work includes the Marvel Knights relaunch of *The Punisher*, as well as *Punisher/Wolverine: Revelation*, and Wildstorm's *Night Tribes*. His other work includes stints on *The Crow*, *Spider-Man Unlimited*, *Buffy the Vampire Slayer*, and the one-shot *Blade: Crescent City Blues*.

Before becoming a full-time writer, he was licensing manager for *Billboard* magazine in New York, where he worked on Fox Television's *Billboard Music Awards* and *American Top 40* radio, among many other projects.

Golden was born and raised in Massachusetts, where he still lives with his family. He graduated from Tufts University. He has recently completed a new, original dark fantasy entitled *Strangewood*, which will be published in September 1999. Please visit him at www.christophergolden.com.

BUFFY

THE VAMPIRE

SLAYER™

As long as there have been vampires, there has been the Slayer.
One girl in all the world, to find them where they gather and
to stop the spread of their evil and the swell of their numbers

Child of the Hunt
Return to Chaos
Obsidian Fate

The Gatekeeper Trilogy:
Out of the Madhouse
Ghost Roads
Sons of Entropy

The Watcher's Guide

Based on the hit TV series created by Joss Whedon

Published by Pocket Books

POCKET
BOOKS   1998 Twentieth Century Fox Film Corporation. All Right Reserved.

2022-02

Dawson's Creek ™

Trouble in Paradise
An ALL-NEW, ORIGINAL STORY
Featuring the characters of Dawson's Creek

Here comes trouble...

To promote fall tourism, Capeside has a new slogan, "Fall in Love in Capeside," and a new weekend romance festival, including a kissing marathon. Pacey can't wait, but Andie's not interested. Then there's the contest for best romantic video that Dawson's dying to win, if only he could decide who should get the female lead.

Jen's visiting cousin Courtney might be just right for the role. She's not acting mean anymore. She's actually...nice. *Way* too nice, think Joey and Jen. And their instincts are right, because when Courtney starts scheming, watch out Capeside!

Based on the hit television show produced by Columbia TriStar Television

Published by Pocket Books

In time of tragedy,
a love that would not die...

Hindenburg, 1937
By Cameron Dokey

San Francisco Earthquake, 1906
By Kathleen Duey

Chicago Fire, 1871
By Elizabeth Massie

Washington Avalanche, 1910
By Cameron Dokey

---

sweeping stories of star-crossed romance

Starting in July 1999

From Archway Paperbacks
Published by Pocket Books

Buffy: "Willow, why don't you compile a list of kids who've died here who might have turned into ghosts."

Xander: "We're on a Hellmouth. It's gonna be a long list."

Willow: "Have you seen the 'In Memorium' section in the yearbook?"

BUFFY

THE VAMPIRE

SLAYER™

How *does* the Sunnydale yearbook staff memorialize all the less fortunate classmates?

Get your very own copy of the Slayer's Sunnydale High School yearbook, full of cast photos, school event wrap-ups, and personal notes from Buffy's best buds.

THE SUNNYDALE HIGH YEARBOOK

By Christopher Golden and Nancy Holder

Available Fall 1999

Published by Pocket Books